TARGET *for* REVENGE

Marlene Chase

Annie's®
AnniesFiction.com

Library of Congress-in-Publication Data
Target for Revenge / by Marlene Chase
p. cm.
I. Title
                    2016900360

AnniesFiction.com
(800) 282-6643
Secrets of the Quilt™
Series Creator: Shari Lohner
Series Editors: Shari Lohner, Janice Tate, and Ken Tate
Cover Illustrator: Jonathan Bouw

10 11 12 13 14 | Printed in China | 9 8 7 6 5 4 3 2

"You who live your lives in cities or among peaceful ways cannot always tell whether your friends are the kind who would go through fire for you. But on the Plains one's friends have an opportunity to prove their mettle."
—*Buffalo Bill Cody*

1

Omaha, Nebraska
June 1885

The elegant carriage, powered by two sleek horses with flowing black manes, rolled past the train station and the expanding city of Omaha and out into the Nebraska countryside. Elizabeth Carson clutched her beaded reticule in her lap, hardly able to contain her excitement. She threw back her head and breathed deeply of air so sweet and fragrant that it made her almost giddy. The wind tugged at the strings of her bonnet and blew curly tendrils of auburn hair around her face.

She turned to her sister, who sat next to her on the leather-backed seat. "Oh Meg, I can't believe we're finally here. It's going to be the most wonderful summer of our lives!"

The sparkle in Meg's hazel eyes matched the excitement in her sister's dancing chocolate ones. "We really are a long way from Boston, aren't we, Libby?" she said, using the nickname she'd given her sister and sweeping her arms out in a broad arc. "I've never seen so much open space."

Libby scanned the landscape, so different from the urban sprawl they were used to. The prairie—unfenced, undivided, unmeasured except for varying tints of grass or grain—yawned on both sides of the dusty road. Vast stretches of wheat shimmered beneath an azure sky trailing pink and gold ribbons in the waning day. Here and there, a lone tree rose like a hermit in the wilderness as cattle grazed nearby.

"It's magnificent, isn't it?" she breathed. "This land is like a great ocean."

Meg shivered though the air was mild and pressed closer to her older sister. "It makes me feel so small, this endless prairie." She shook her head slowly. "Can you believe Aunt Tillie, a proper lady from London, really lives here in this wild country?"

Libby tucked her sister's hand in hers. "I suppose it is wild, but I've heard such remarkable things about people who headed west to make their fortunes here." She smiled, feeling grateful to be alive.

Indeed, they were a long way from home. They had spent the last year at the academy for young ladies, learning all the things young women were supposed to learn in order to be successful. *Success ultimately means finding a suitable husband*, Libby thought with a sigh. It wasn't that she didn't want to marry someday and raise a family, but so many exciting things were happening in the world.

Women were achieving prominence in fields quite apart from marriage, like Miss Clara Barton, the pioneer nurse who established the American Red Cross. Silently, Libby applauded the shy educator who had tended wounded soldiers on some of the grimmest battlefields of the Civil War. How tenderly she had brought light and healing during the sieges of Petersburg and Richmond.

She also admired Amelia Bloomer, suffrage pioneer and writer. Women could be and do much more than some had ever thought possible. There was so much to discover, so much to try beyond the small circle of the elite New England community in which she had been raised. And she, Elizabeth Jane Carson, and her sister, Margaret, were going to see something new and exciting in the strange and rapidly expanding West.

"Can you believe Mother let us come when Aunt Tillie invited us?" Meg asked, her fair complexion growing rosy. "She had great plans for the season back home, with colorful parties filled with men vying for your hand."

"I suppose Mother's afraid we'll become old maids," Libby said, laughing. "As if that is the absolute worst thing that could ever happen to a girl."

Meg sighed. "Well, I don't think I should like it very much," she said thoughtfully, wrinkling her short nose. "I might have to worry about spinsterhood, but not you."

There was no bitterness in her comment, Libby knew. No one was more loyal than Meg or more complimentary, praising Libby's dramatic coloring, her mysterious dark eyes and shiny hair, as well as her adventurous spirit that sometimes got them both in trouble. Like the time they'd put their little brother's pet frog in fussy old Uncle Horace's bedchamber. His shouts of protest must have been heard for miles across Boston Common. The next morning at breakfast, he had announced that he would have to return early to Amherst. Libby smiled at the memory. Uncle Horace's early leave-taking had been a blessing, in everyone's estimation.

Meg seemed unaware of her own merits—her quiet, discerning spirit, her warmth and humility. She had physical charms as well—silken hair the color of ripening wheat and large eyes of a color one could never quite label. Sometimes they were green, sometimes brown, and often they were many shades in between. It occurred to Libby now that Meg's eyes were very like the colors of the prairie through which they were passing.

"I daresay someone will scoop you up first, sister," Libby said. "You would make any man proud, but there *are* things more desirable than finding a husband." She pursed her lips thoughtfully. Many of her friends were planning weddings while she, at twenty-one, had no serious prospects despite her mother's frequent matchmaking. It would be nice to be free of those games for a while.

As the carriage picked up speed, Libby felt her spirit soar. They were going to see the West, at least as far west as Nebraska. There would be cowboys, Indians, maybe even a gunfight or two. She had read about the western outlaw Jesse James, who only a year or two ago had been shot to death by Robert Ford, a member of his own band. Robert and his brother, Charles, had been recruited to rob the Platte City Bank, but they had opted to collect the $10,000 reward for their infamous leader instead.

It had also been just a few years since the famous gunfight at the O.K. Corral took place in Tombstone, Arizona. It was thrilling in a strange way to read about the exploits of Doc Holliday, Wyatt Earp, and his brothers Morgan and Virgil. The West was a dangerous territory.

But we're perfectly safe, she thought with some disappointment, for Mother had planned carefully for any possible contingency. Aunt Tillie had promised they would be properly chaperoned and taken to all the best gatherings in the growing civilization of Omaha, Nebraska.

History fascinated Libby, so she had scrambled to learn everything she could about the wild country they were about to experience. She knew that Nebraska was crossed by many historic trails explored by Meriwether Lewis and William Clark and that the California Gold Rush of 1849 had brought the first large numbers of nonindigenous settlers to the area. Rapid development ensued, especially after Omaha had been declared the eastern terminus of a transcontinental railroad.

"I can't wait to get to Aunt Tillie's homestead," Libby said, turning to nineteen-year-old Meg with excitement. "Everything is so different."

The burly driver Aunt Tillie had hired to meet them turned

around on the raised seat of the carriage. He had a weather-reddened face and a gray mustache that curved around his mouth and flipped up at the ends. "You ladies all right back there?" he asked over his leather-clad shoulder. His broad western hat didn't budge an inch as they rumbled through the countryside. Libby supposed all men in the West wore cowboy hats, even with their Sunday best.

"We're fine, sir," Libby responded.

"Won't be too long now, ladies." And he urged the horses onward with a quick snap of his whip that didn't quite reach the animals' rumps. "Soon you'll be tucked up in Tillie's feather beds."

They had traveled for days by rail, and though the seats of the train could be made into reasonably comfortable berths for sleeping, the journey had been long and arduous. Another few miles of prairie and they would arrive at Aunt Tillie's homestead. Libby was tired, but her mind took in every detail around her. "A person can do anything, be anyone, in this wild, wonderful country," she said excitedly. "The very air smells of freedom."

Meg's tawny head soon drooped and fell lightly on Libby's shoulder. It had been a wearying journey, but Libby felt alive in every nerve. Every fiber of her soul resonated with the beauty and scope of the world around her. She couldn't help expressing her thoughts, whether Meg was awake or not.

"I think our Aunt Tillie is very brave," she said, imagining their first sight of her in this strange land. "Especially now that Uncle Hector is gone and she's by herself." Indeed, she could have gone back to London or Boston, perhaps married again, but she stayed right there on the land her husband had claimed. "She's a real pioneer," Libby breathed. "Imagine fighting off disease, hunger, and marauding bands of Indians to gain a start in a brand-new country—this country!"

Meg's head bobbed up. "Do you think we'll see any Indians?"

"Don't be silly," Libby said. "They're all on reservations now. They aren't allowed to wander around free. The Sioux were the last holdouts, but cold and hunger forced them to return to the U.S. from Canada and surrender." She shook her head sadly, not wanting to think about the terror that arose from westward expansion as Native Americans were gradually forced off their land, their resources depleted.

"What's that?" Meg queried, her eyes suddenly wide with alarm.

Rounding a bend in the road, they were met with a startling sight. A host of tents and teepees were spread across an immense area in the distance.

"Is it a reservation?" Libby asked loudly of the carriage driver, who seemed unconcerned and continued toward the dwellings.

"Don't fret, ladies," the man said, slowing slightly and making a half-turn toward them. "That's Colonel Cody's Wild West show, where the sharpshooters and rough riders reenact battles. Those teepees belong to the Indians he hires to make a rip-roaring show. They perform from city to city and bring folks in from all around."

Libby was intrigued. "Isn't he that famous Indian scout who got the Medal of Honor some years back?"

"That's him. Buffalo Bill Cody. He was a civilian scout, but everyone calls him Colonel. He hired Indians from the reservations to put on pretend battles like the ones he fought himself. Hasn't been at it long. He started right here in Nebraska." The driver swung his bulk back around to focus on the road. "The Colonel attracts a lot of attention, but everyone ain't happy about it. Folks got long memories when it comes to Indian raids."

They were drawing closer to the tenting area, which was set back from the road at a considerable distance. Libby could make out horses and buffalo in the field and see smoke from campfires.

"Oh, could we stop for a little while?" she begged. "I've never seen real teepees."

"Do you think we should, Libby?" Meg was fully awake now and peering into the distance at the panoramic view.

"We need to stretch our legs. We've been riding for such a long time." Libby leaned as far forward as she could and appealed to the driver. He'd been hired to serve them, after all, and should accede to their wishes. "We'd like to walk a little, if you don't mind, to get a closer look."

At Libby's request, he pulled back on the reins. He jumped down from the high seat with a grace that belied his considerable bulk. Libby drew back the skirt of her organdy traveling dress and was out the carriage door as soon as the driver opened it.

They walked along the road, the driver leading the horses and following a few yards behind. The light was dusky now, the sun preparing to set over the vast prairie. Libby stared in wonder at the scene beyond them. "Look at all those tents and teepees. Imagine building a house out of poles and animal skins. I've read that they're warm in winter and cool in summer, and they can be dissembled quickly when they want to move on. Aren't they marvelous?"

Suddenly Meg stopped. "Libby!"

Libby tore her eyes away from the riveting scene ahead and looked into Meg's ashen face.

"There's something in the ditch there," she whispered, "across the road."

The girls crossed to the other side and walked silently toward what appeared to be a man lying on his back. He looked as if he might be sleeping. As they advanced, the figure remained motionless.

"Good heavens, Libby. He looks like—"

"It's an Indian!"

The figure on the ground wore a great headdress of feathers and a buckskin tunic heavily trimmed with colorful beads. A leather bag hung at his side and a crucifix lay askew across his chest. A blanket was crumpled a yard or so away from him.

Stepping yet closer, Libby gasped. "There's blood under that headdress. He's been hurt." She sprang forward and knelt over him. She searched the deeply bronzed face, the stern features fixed in an expression of proud repose. He was beautiful and frightening. Her pulse raced and her breath caught in her throat.

Meg knelt down beside Libby. "Is he . . . ?"

"Quick, Meg. Get my wrap."

Meg raced to the carriage and pulled Libby's blue silk shawl from a valise.

The carriage driver had reached Libby's side and was looking down at the man, frowning. "It's one of Cody's Indians," he said. "Best to leave him be. You never know what these savages might—"

"Water! Get some water!" Libby cried. "This man needs help."

The driver reluctantly went back to the carriage and returned with a leather canteen. Libby poured water over one end of her expensive Turkish shawl and gently dabbed at the trickles of blood that flowed from a wound on his head onto the man's deeply lined face. Beneath his headdress, graying black hair hung in a long, thick plait. He looked as old as the earth but probably wasn't more than fifty or sixty, judging from his muscled body.

The wound didn't appear serious. As Libby stroked his forehead with the cool fabric, his breathing grew more even. When he stirred slightly, Libby held her breath, torn between concern and fear. Was he dangerous? Had he fallen and hit his head? Had he been attacked? Was he drunk?

She knew that the sale of alcohol had been prohibited for American Indians for quite some time. Now, twenty-four years later, no one was allowed to brew or sell intoxicating liquors. But greedy men often circumvented laws for their own gain—and to the detriment of the innocent. She sniffed but smelled no spirits on him.

Who was he? How long had he been able to hunt buffalo and move untroubled across land that had been home to his people? Did he have a family, children whom he taught the old ways? Something in the proud old face moved her.

When his eyes flicked suddenly open, she whispered, "It's all right. We're here to help."

His dark gaze grew wide with some unnamed emotion or passion. Was it fear—or anger? She leaned down lower to help him up, but he glared at her and made a jerky sweep of his hand, a shooing gesture that was clearly a refusal of assistance. Did he think they were the ones who hurt him? That they were his enemies?

Suddenly, he rolled onto his side and scrambled to his feet with an ease surprising for his age, height, and injury. He adjusted the great headdress of feathers. Was he a real chief, or was he simply playing a part in the western show?

"You've been hurt," Libby said, swallowing hard. "But we have a carriage. We can take you home."

The man drew himself up even taller and crossed his buckskin-covered arms across his chest. He glowered down at her, his sculpted features hard as red clay.

Libby's breath caught. Would he turn on them? Use that sharp-looking knife snugged to his leg? All the harrowing tales of Indian raids on hapless settlers came streaming through her mind in living color.

The Indian backed away from them, making a grunting sound. Two harsh syllables fell on the gathering night. "I walk." He turned and headed for the distant teepees, his feet in leather moccasins making no sound at all on the dusty earth.

2

Omaha, Nebraska
June 1885

Tillie Primm stood as Libby and Meg entered the kitchen. She cut a commanding figure in a gown of gold and black stripes, a tall, large-boned woman without an ounce of fat to be seen. A morning shawl, held in place with a handsome oval brooch, draped her broad shoulders. Behind her, the sun streaming through the window shone on salt-and-pepper hair caught in a neat bun. Her no-nonsense aspect was gentled by a humorous glint in dark, probing eyes. The table before her was spread with a white linen cloth and a surprising assortment of fine china and crystal.

A good-size black poodle that had been curled in Aunt Tillie's lap now stood at her side. Aunt Tillie smiled broadly, revealing even white teeth and a dimple in her rounded chin. "My dear Libby and Meg! Come in, come in. I hope you slept well."

She had welcomed them with great enthusiasm the night before, tucked them into bed with fluffy quilts, and said they should sleep as long as they wished. The ranch hands would be fed outside under the elms at six a.m., but they were to "pay them no mind."

Libby went to her aunt and kissed her smooth, round cheek. Tillie was in her midfifties and light of complexion, with wrinkles confined to the corners of her eyes. Clearly, she avoided the hot summer sun and was wealthy enough to hire others to do the kind of work that could age a woman. *I haven't seen her since I was ten, but she's hardly changed at all,* Libby thought. *Still formidable, buoyant, and never at a loss for words.*

"Greta, do bring some fresh pancakes for my favorite nieces," Tillie said in a kind but authoritative voice. She signaled a fortyish woman who stood at the stove, wearing a white apron atop her homespun dress. "Girls, this is Mrs. Bergstrom, the best cook in this part of the country."

Greta glanced at her mistress with surprise and quick pleasure. She was short and plump with pale blue eyes and platinum hair wound into a braided circle. *This must be the helper Aunt Tillie mentioned in her letters,* Libby thought. She'd hired the widowed Norwegian woman as a live-in caretaker after Greta's husband had died of cholera, leaving her and her daughter destitute. *Mrs. Bergstrom is a passable cook, even if she can't speak English,* Tillie had written her sister. It seemed clear that they had worked out an amenable, if not friendly, relationship. The compliment about her cooking might have sealed the affection between the two of them.

"Pleased to meet," Greta said softly, dropping the pronoun in her thick Scandinavian English.

"And where is Sonja?" Aunt Tillie asked.

"She brings breakfast tins from the menfolk. She comes now."

A striking girl of seventeen or eighteen stepped inside the big ranch kitchen. She stopped in midstep at the sight of company and set several tin containers on the floor. Light brown eyes enhanced her rosy complexion and complemented hair as blond as her mother's.

"My nieces. Elizabeth, and the hungry one there is Margaret," Aunt Tillie said glowingly. "They've had a very long trip, all the way from Boston. I'm pleased to say they'll be staying with us this summer."

Sonja Bergstrom smiled shyly, glancing from Libby to Meg with genuine interest. She bobbed her head in a kind of curtsy that made Libby vaguely uncomfortable.

Libby exchanged glances with Meg, who was somewhat undaintily digging into a stack of golden pancakes. "We're very happy to make your acquaintance. And it's quite all right to call us Libby and Meg." She glanced apologetically at Aunt Tillie.

Aunt Tillie was a very proper woman, reared to observe class distinctions, and in New England, she had enjoyed life in high-society circles. After being left a childless widow by her first husband, she had married Hector Primm, her rancher husband and distant cousin, late in life. She had returned with him to Nebraska, bringing along many of the fine things she had collected over the years along with the social customs with which she'd grown up. It occurred to Libby that her aunt's married name, Primm, was quite apt.

When Hector passed away only three years after their marriage, everyone had thought Tillie would give up life on the plains and go back East. It couldn't be easy to live on the prairie, though much had improved since Hector, fifteen years older than Tillie, had taken advantage of the Homestead Act, signed into law by President Abraham Lincoln in 1862.

For a filing fee of eighteen dollars, Hector had purchased fifty of the millions of acres of land that were eventually turned over to private citizens. Settlers had to live on the land, build a home, make improvements, and farm for five years before becoming full and legal owners. Determined and hardy, the pioneers carved out a life and a civilization. They raised children, broke land, planted farms, and dug wells in the midst of the tallgrass prairies of the Great Plains.

The homes they built were made of tough prairie sod piled into walls with openings for windows and doors. Their sod houses, often called "soddies," were chiseled out of the hillsides and were comfortably warm in winter and cool in summer.

In 1884, Aunt Tillie's homestead on the outskirts of Omaha was a handsome, whitewashed brick building with real glazed windows and painted shutters. The house was laid out on one floor and had a large kitchen, a parlor big enough to host a ball, and three roomy bedrooms, one of which was occupied by Greta.

Tillie had been alone for nearly eight years now, but Hector had left her well established on the homestead. Tillie herself had received a generous bequest from her first marriage that no doubt had helped Hector develop his land more quickly than could have been accomplished by most settlers. She was his second wife, the first having succumbed to pneumonia in her thirties and without bearing children. Tillie had likewise been unable to give birth, a sadness that sometimes came through in her letters, which overall were filled with glowing reports of life on the plains.

"I am so thrilled to have you here," Tillie said. "My dear Elizabeth and Margaret, what beautiful young ladies you have become. That finishing school my sister arranged for you has done you proud, I must say."

Before they could respond, Aunt Tillie addressed Sonja in her more imperious voice reserved for nonfamily members. "We'll need more sausage from the smokehouse. Go along and bring a full rope." When Sonja and her mother departed from the kitchen, Tillie turned to Libby. "Now, my dears, tell me all your news. The balls in Boston, are they still as grand as I remember them?"

Libby paused to sip her tea. At such events, girls were expected to present themselves in their best fashion as prospects for eligible young men. She hadn't found these parties "grand" so much as tedious. She would rather read or play the piano or do almost anything else. "I expect they are, Aunt Tillie," Libby said resignedly, but she could think of nothing more to say on the matter.

"They had a delightful celebration for the new bridge," Meg put in. She had learned to make up in the areas where Libby had a lack. "It's called the New York and Brooklyn Bridge."

"You don't say!" Tillie responded. "I heard it had finally been completed. That German, Roebling, must have been a genius to build a bridge that spans such a distance. I understand his wife, Emily, was the first to cross it. That would be something to celebrate." She laughed heartily and slipped a crust of bread to the poodle sitting by her chair. "Duchess is very fond of soda bread, aren't you, darling?"

Libby had followed the story of how Washington Roebling had conducted the entire construction of the great bridge, designing and redesigning caissons and other equipment after the death of his father, John. What was most exciting to Libby was how Emily Warren Roebling had provided the critical written link between her husband and the engineers on the site.

"Mrs. Roebling studied higher mathematics, bridge specifications, and cable construction," Libby said. "Then she spent more than a decade helping to supervise the bridge's construction."

Tillie lifted an eyebrow and gave Libby an appraising look. "You don't say." She dropped another piece of bread to the waiting Duchess, who nibbled it daintily. "So this ball to celebrate the bridge, was it a very grand affair?"

"Oh yes," Meg said. "And Libby had the eye of every gentleman in the room." She nudged her sister with her elbow.

"I don't doubt it," Tillie said, appraising both of her nieces with pride. "And I do hope those trunks the driver hefted from the carriage last night contain some pretty gowns, because I am going to introduce you to some of the West's finest." Her eyes glinted with excitement. "I can't wait to show you off. In fact, there's a tea to celebrate the mayor's first term in office this afternoon at three, right here in our parlor."

"Aunt Tillie, you don't have to worry about entertaining us," Libby said.

"Certainly not," Meg put in. "We're happy to be here, and we'd like to see everything in this wild country. The cowboys and Indians and all."

"You've been reading those frightful dime novels by Ned Buntline," Tillie said, laughing. "Cowboys and Indians indeed! We're much more civilized here in Nebraska." She pushed back from the table and called to Greta. They all moved out of Greta's way as she bustled in and cleared the dishes away.

"And see that Duchess gets some milk," Tillie told Greta. "Duchess is in a family way, so we're spoiling her," she added with a chuckle.

"Oh," said Libby, patting the dog's curly head. "Will the puppies be born soon? I hope we get to see them."

"Very soon by the look of her," Tillie said.

"But we *did* see a real Indian," Meg broke in, refusing to be deterred from their wild adventure of the night before. "He had a huge headdress of feathers and a fearsome countenance. He was hurt; there was blood from a gash on his head. We got him some water, and Libby wiped his face with her shawl." Meg's eyes shone with golden light. "We would have had the driver take him home, but the Indian got up and walked away."

"That sounds like a dream, dear." Tillie frowned and brushed crumbs from her dress. "The Indians are all on reservations now."

"The carriage driver told us that he was probably part of the western show that a man called Cody runs," Libby said, recalling the blood on the Indian's fierce but marvelous face and the anguish in his eyes. "I believe he was unconscious when we came upon him in the road."

Tillie put a ringed finger to her jaw and tapped it thoughtfully. "That rowdy show. I must say I'm not in favor of it, though our esteemed mayor, God bless him, thinks it might attract more people to our city and bring in revenue."

"You should have seen the tents and teepees, the horses and huge buffalo!" Meg exulted. "We made the driver stop so we could get a look at it all."

"Hardly a place for refined young ladies," Tillie said emphatically. "I suppose it's all right for roustabouts and folk who haven't been exposed to real culture." She laughed, which took some of the sting from her words. Then, impulsively, she drew both girls to her ample bosom and hugged them. "Run along now and unpack. Greta will assist you with any pressing and such, and think about what to wear for the social." She clasped her hands. "Something simple but elegant for the afternoon. Our new mayor will be in attendance, and if we're lucky, the handsome Robert Ealy too."

Libby suppressed a groan. Aunt Tillie was too much like Mother when it came to matchmaking. "Aunt Tillie, do you suppose we could look around first, maybe see the horses and all after we've unpacked?"

"Well, of course you can. Ain't that much to see besides acres of corn and wheat, the herd, and chickens."

Libby smiled to hear a word like "ain't" from her sophisticated aunt. *Some of the so-called inferior Nebraska culture must be rubbing off.*

"Teddy, the lad I hired to take care of the stock, will show you around. You'll find him either out tending the plow horses or in his niche in the barn. The other hired hands live in the bunkhouse, but Teddy's made a place for himself in the stable."

She stooped to pat Duchess's head, then stretched to her full five feet nine inches. "I must see to arrangements for this afternoon's tea. Greta, you best get started on those raisin cakes."

When they had finished unpacking and laying out their dresses for the soiree, Libby and Meg went in search of Teddy.

The outbuildings were made of the same whitewashed brick as Tillie's home and had been placed a good distance away. All of them, including the privy, were neat, if somewhat primitive, in appearance. It was a testament to Aunt Tillie's prosperity that she had a privy. But it was the land itself that Libby found breathtaking. Beyond the cleared area around the homestead lay miles and miles of cultivated land as well as untouched prairie, its grasses waving in the light summer wind. They continued along the narrow path toward the stable and saw horses ahead in the corral, grazing and stamping magnificently behind the rail fence.

"Aren't they beautiful?" Libby exclaimed to Meg. Gathering up her skirts, she hurried forward. Upon reaching the rail fence, she hefted herself up to watch. There were a few draft horses, but others, more sleek and lithe, looked like they were born for the saddle. "I bet the cowboys use them to chase stray cattle or rope calves," she said. "I'd love to watch them in action."

"Look at that one. He shines like the sunset." Meg leaned against the fence, her eyes wide with delight. "A golden palomino."

"I wonder where the young man is who takes care of these beauties," Libby mused.

You'll recognize Teddy, Aunt Tillie had told them before they left the house. *Hair the color of carrots and a field of copper freckles.*

Libby smiled. He sounded like their little brother, who had similar features. Likely the ranch hand with the innocent-sounding name was out branding cattle or in the barn, doing his chores.

"Don't move!" a threatening voice behind them commanded.

Libby turned to see a man in boots and a wide-brimmed hat wielding a gun. She froze. Were they to be killed by some outlaw right here on their Aunt Tillie's property? On the first day of their summer holiday? But there was no more time to think—only a second to register her panic, because the gun suddenly exploded in the summer air.

3

Cabot Falls, Vermont
Present Day

The gaunt man known as Howahkan took Sofia's business card and tucked it into the pocket of his suede jacket. He emerged from her car without a word, giving only the barest nod of his head in response to her wish for a good night's rest. She promised that she would return the next afternoon to take him to the library for the annual Cabot Falls Art Show.

Sofia watched with puzzled disappointment as the talented Native American painter walked to the door of the inn where she had preregistered him for Wednesday through Saturday. *This doesn't look good.*

As the chairperson of the art show committee, she was charged with the special guest's care during his stay in their town. She had been impressed with his work that featured expansive desert scenes, buffalo roaming vast prairies, and portraits of Native Americans, their faces etched with nobility and anguish. On her recommendation, and after reading reviews of his western paintings, the committee had invited him to be the featured artist.

Sofia's first view of him had startled her. The tall thirty-something man had shiny hair pulled into a long black ponytail, which was doubled under and fastened with a gold clip at the nape of his neck. In the promotional photograph, his hip-length hair hung loose in undulating waves.

His warrior-like face, though sharply angular with a prominent nose, seemed less fierce than delicate. He was remarkably handsome, or might have been if the faintest hint of humor or light touched his deep-set eyes, which were light brown, like his skin.

Attempts at conversation during the ride from the airport to the inn had fallen flat. Howahkan avoided her eyes and ignored her questions or seemed not to hear them. Language couldn't be the problem. He'd studied at a good art university and had lived in New York for more than a decade. So what was wrong? Why did he appear sad to the point of being morose?

It had been a long flight, delayed due to fog in the Boston area, and the artist was likely tired, she supposed. Soon he would be expected to mingle and discuss his work with interested guests at the show. It was part of the agreement she had worked out with his agent. But from the moment she'd introduced herself, she'd hardly gotten a word out of him. *Some attraction he's going to be!*

Nothing had worked out the way Sofia had planned that day. The morning had been hectic, the kids especially needy. Vanessa couldn't find her purple sweater. Matthew insisted that Sofia had forgotten to sign his homework. Wynter had them all scrambling to find her geography book at the last minute. Luke had been sent back to his room to change twice. Pajama bottoms might be the in thing among his peers, but they were out as far as she was concerned, especially for school.

Her friends Julie and Marla, for all their usual helpfulness and skill, hadn't finished the signs for the show. She had had to do that in the morning, and then her afternoon art classes had gone on longer than usual. After school she transported the kids to this and that, made the tiramisu, set out an early dinner, and answered a host of texts and phone calls about the art show.

She couldn't fault Marla and Julie, who had provided fabulous support preparing for the show; they had busy lives too. A widow in her late forties, Marla Dixon was quiet by nature but full of a zest for life that she poured into everything she undertook. Marla worked at the Cabot Falls Public Library and had a son to guide through the treacherous waters of adolescence. Her lean, athletic build testified to her love of the outdoors, which was often reflected in her paintings. She and Sofia, along with Julie Butler, were the three members of an art club called the Pinot Painters.

Unlike Marla, Julie was chatty and boisterous. Now in her early forties, she had twin daughters who enjoyed fancy nail painting almost as much as their mother did. Between her family duties and her full-time work in marketing at a public relations firm, she was lucky to have any energy to spare for community projects.

Howahkan had been expected to arrive at six, which would have allowed plenty of time for Sofia to get home and do a quick pickup of the house. But as fate would have it, he'd been two hours late. Time she desperately needed to get ready for her sisters' arrival was spent hanging around the airport. Sofia was throwing a posthumous birthday celebration for Nonna, with coffee, dessert, and a look at the quilt Nonna had willed to Sofia. *What was I thinking, having a party with Rosa and Gina the night before the art show?*

She sped toward home as the unforgiving clock on the dashboard marched annoyingly on. Rosa Scipione, her eldest sister, an astrophysicist, had cleared her busy schedule at Cornell University. She and her heart-surgeon husband moved in important circles and guarded their precious time.

Gina McCray, though not quite the stickler for punctuality that her older sister was, nonetheless didn't suffer fools gladly. She had her Ph.D. in microbiology and taught at Boston University. She would no doubt wonder why her stay-at-home sister who had only a household to run couldn't manage her time more efficiently.

Sofia tried unsuccessfully to shake her dark mood and wondered if Howahkan's morose personality was catching. Seeing Jim at the door, however, heartened her.

Her husband had exchanged his plaid flannel shirt for an open-collared cotton one and had smoothed his thick blond hair in honor of the visit from his sisters-in-law. His rugged, all-American face shone with understanding and respect. But for all his easygoing friendliness, he could make his math students tremble if they tried to put anything over on him.

She loved coming home and finding Jim waiting for her, though he seldom stood sentinel at the front door. She sighed, knowing why he was there now.

"Your sisters are here," he announced. He moved aside to usher her in. "Ready and waiting," he added with a warning dancing in his blue eyes. While he was fond of his wife's family, he often made himself scarce around Rosa and Gina, who were loud and larger than life. They could be overbearing at times and hot-tempered when challenged.

Sofia stepped into the living room where Vanessa was showing her Aunt Rosa the latest illustrations in her sketchbook. Lately her daughter had taken to drawing long, lean models in unique designer clothing. Launching into a description of an elegant evening gown, she tossed her shoulder-length blond hair and leaned over her aunt's shoulder.

"I call it 'Evening in Paris,'" she said airily. "The long silk scarf floats in the breeze as she walks along the Champs-Élysées, and every head turns in her direction."

Tall, thin Rosa looked much like one of the charcoal sketches herself. She was dressed in a navy pinstripe suit accented with a red paisley scarf, her black hair neatly drawn back. She was tapping her slim left foot, a sign of impatience.

Sofia hurried to embrace her older sister, at the same time catching sight of a clutter of toy cars on the sofa. "Matthew, put those away. We need the room to sit." She kissed Rosa's smooth, olive-tone cheek. "I'm sorry to be late. The guest artist for our show arrived today, and I was chosen to transport him from the airport."

She turned to greet Gina, who was admiring Matthew's cars. "I thought his plane would never get here," she added breathlessly. "And who would think there would be a traffic jam in little Cabot Falls?"

Rosa narrowed her dark eyes, another indication that she was irked at being kept waiting. "We're glad you made it. We were beginning to wonder if you'd forgotten us."

"Don't badger the poor girl." Gina jumped up from the couch to give Sofia a hug.

Rosa relented and smiled at her sisters. "We haven't been waiting too long."

"And Jim's been supplying us with some absolutely to-die-for coffee. What is that flavor?" Gina glanced around.

Sofia smiled, knowing that Jim had absconded the minute she'd arrived. Still, he'd entertained them in her absence, for which she was grateful. "Smells like almond mocha," she said, wondering how that would go with tiramisu. She turned to her younger daughter. "Wynter, will you start dishing up the dessert? I'm going to change." She turned to address her sisters. "I won't be a moment, I promise."

She hurried upstairs, glad for a moment to collect both her wits and the quilt that would be part of the tribute to their grandmother, Elena "Nonna" Baresi. *A posthumous birthday party. Why not?* Nonna had been special in all their lives, full of spunk and surprises. Born in Italy, she had moved to the United States when she was twelve and built a full life with a husband and six children, one of whom was Sofia's mother, Celeste.

The truth was, Sofia could barely remember her mother because she was so young when Celeste had died in a car accident. Nonna had become both mother and family matriarch in one formidable package.

Nonna had made every gathering come alive with her expansive personality and her vibrant eyes that lightened even the darkest corner. Sofia missed her terribly.

Sofia always felt like something of a misfit in the family, but Nonna had championed her individuality. Rosa and Gina were smart, ambitious, and competitive, with their advanced science degrees. But Sofia had chosen to pursue her creative passions and had earned a degree in studio art.

After she met Jim and had kids, she found that she loved being a stay-at-home mom. She still enjoyed painting and giving art lessons, but since her kids had gotten older, she was turning her talent for cooking into a profession with some catering jobs here and there. Her creative talents, however, didn't extend to needle and thread.

Neither of her sisters quite understood why Nonna had willed the priceless heirloom quilt in its beautiful hand-carved trunk to her. Both Rosa and Gina had finely developed needlework skills, a testament to Nonna's careful tutoring. But Sofia could barely manage an even row of stitches, much less the fine hand quilting her sisters accomplished.

Sofia sat on the edge of the bed, looked at the trunk, and sighed. It scared her to be the caretaker of such a valuable family treasure, even though she knew how to properly protect the quilt and was reminded regularly by Rosa. It was wrapped in cotton fabric to protect it from dust, light, and abrasion. She laundered the cotton wrapping yearly to remove any dust or acid that built up in it. She also refolded the quilt frequently to prevent permanent creases and redistribute the batting.

Now she carefully lifted the quilt out of the trunk. She'd learned a lot from Nonna's bequest, but why she had inherited it still baffled her. Rosa was the one whose stitching was an absolute marvel to behold, whose design sense was amazing. She should have been the one chosen.

Comfortable in her jeans and a light sweatshirt, Sofia carried the quilt into the four-season room adjoining the kitchen. The large rectangular table would be perfect for laying out the heirloom once a clean white sheet was spread over its surface. That was exactly what Jim was doing as she came into the room.

He turned his handsome face to her as he pulled the sheet even. She had simply mentioned at breakfast the need to prepare a table for the quilt, but Jim hadn't forgotten. Sometimes she wondered why she was so lucky to have been gifted with such a thoughtful and supportive husband.

"You remembered," she said softly and lifted her face to his. With her arms full of quilt, she kissed him. "And thanks for making coffee." In a whisper only he could hear, she added, "You saved me."

He chuckled and gave a low bow. "My pleasure, ma'am." He winked and strode toward the door. "And now, if you'll excuse me, I'm going upstairs to grade math quizzes."

Sofia set the quilt down carefully and went to help Wynter bring the plates of tiramisu into the living room, where Vanessa was pouring more coffee into Sofia's best china cups.

"Can we go now?" Wynter asked, setting two plates down on the coffee table. "Vanessa's going to help me with my English homework. We're supposed to write a poem." She screwed up her nose and rolled her eyes in an expression that clearly described her commentary on the assignment.

Sofia thanked her daughters and joined her sisters, who were discussing diets as only two scientists could.

"Grains as a staple food is best," Rosa said. "Supplement with vegetables, but nix all that processed and refined stuff."

"You need diversity for a healthy diet," Gina said, although she had been trying her whole life to balance her love of food with her scientific ideals. Unlike her willowy sister, she was decidedly disadvantaged at five feet one inch and perpetually on a diet.

Sofia smiled. Things hadn't changed much over the years. In spite of her weariness and concern about the art show, she was glad her sisters had come. *You don't have to agree on everything to love each other.* "I'm not sure where tiramisu fits into your diets, but we are having a celebration, after all," Sofia said, handing a plate to each of her sisters.

"Of course we are," Rosa said, taking the plate and holding her fork aloft. "Here's to your marvelous tiramisu. And here's to Nonna."

"Yes, to Nonna," Gina said, giving her chin-length auburn hair a toss. "Actually," she said with a grin, "I've decided I'll never get down to my original weight. Seven pounds six ounces isn't realistic."

They laughed and dove heartily into their desserts, each sharing memories of Nonna. Sofia didn't mind when the subject of hand quilting came up. Nonna had worked hard to teach her how to sew, starting with simple embroidery stitches. But Sofia had found them anything but simple. Her heart hadn't been in it.

She was much happier with a paintbrush in her hand, or a piece of charcoal, or a gourmet recipe. These were the artistic pursuits that made the hours fly and her spirit soar. Nonna had understood and gently chastised her sisters if they made comments about her crooked, lumpy stitches.

When the three finished telling stories about their cherished Nonna, they took their dishes to the kitchen and washed their hands.

"I'm excited to see it again," Rosa said. She wiped her hands on a paper towel as she peered into the four-season room where the folded quilt awaited. "Good, you covered the table first."

"You keep it stored in cotton in the trunk, don't you?" Gina shot a conspiratorial glance at Sofia. She often came to her sister's defense when Rosa got a bit high-handed about things.

"I do," Sofia said quietly. Indeed, she had been careful to follow the best guidelines for storing and handling an heirloom quilt. Still, it bothered her to be grilled by family members, some of whom coveted the bequest for themselves and had infinite tidbits of advice on how it ought to be maintained. It came from cousins and aunts mostly, but even Rosa and Gina tried her patience.

Sofia realized that she was feeling cranky, so she made an effort to lighten the moment. "There was that one time I used it for a drop cloth, then I left it out in the rain to get rid of the stains. But it's fine, except for the rip when the neighbor's dog got ahold of it."

Rosa rolled her eyes and Gina laughed.

Crisis averted.

Rosa and Gina tenderly unfolded the quilt and commented on the various pieces. But Sofia's mind was on the art show and specifically on the guest artist for whom she had advocated.

Howahkan's art was unique, distinctively American, and reminiscent of their country's beginnings, when the land was nurtured and buffalo roamed the prairie. What could be more American than someone of native blood? But she worried now that he might not have been the best choice.

Cabot Falls was a small, close-knit community with a quaint charm, rambling woodlands, and sparkling lakes. Citizens and visitors enjoyed the friendly atmosphere of both the businesses and the social gatherings. People who called Cabot Falls home didn't stand on ceremony. They honored frankness and respect, and they trusted one another in a spirit of camaraderie.

They deserved a guest artist who was happy to be there, who would treat them with respect and appreciation. Howahkan, for all of his artistic reputation, wasn't likely to win friends with his taciturn ways.

"What is this?"

Rosa's sharp tone cut through Sofia's anxious thoughts. Rosa was examining a lower left section of the quilt and frowning deeply.

"What's the matter?" Sofia asked, alarmed.

"There's a hole in that lavender swatch." She pointed. "Look for yourself."

"Oh no!" Gina peered over Rosa's shoulder, eyes wide. "What happened?"

Sofia stared at the lovely orchid-toned swatch of silk. Just inside the stitching that joined it to the next piece was a small round hole, slightly brown around one part of the circle. She had never seen it before, and it was small enough to be easily overlooked. Was it a tiny burn hole? It couldn't be from a moth, not with all the precautions she had taken. Besides, she checked the quilt regularly for any hint of infestation.

She felt her sisters' stares, their unspoken accusations. What had she done to mar the beauty of their precious heirloom? Sofia felt her cheeks grow hot. *Oh Nonna*, she mourned without words, *if only you had left the quilt to Rosa or Gina instead of me.* Sofia's heart plummeted. It was a thoroughly dreadful end to a difficult day.

4

Omaha, Nebraska
June 1885

Libby flew off the fence, not sure if she'd jumped or been hit by the bullet, its shot still ringing in her ears.

Meg gave a strangled scream.

They stared transfixed as the man came toward them, gun in hand, eyes on the ground. He stopped a few feet away, and Libby finally saw that his pistol was aimed at a large coiled snake. She looked up and took note of the young man, freckles spread across his short nose, who had saved them.

The man gave the dead snake a push with his boot, lifted a copper eyebrow, and dropped the gun into a leather holster at his hip. "Sorry to scare you," he said. "Gotta watch out for rattlers like that. They like to hide in the tall grass." He cocked his head and smiled. "Theodore Blane, at your service."

Libby gulped air and stared at the unmoving reptile. She heard the anger and panic in her voice as she spoke, but she couldn't stop it. "You scared us half to death!" she yelled, completely forgetting her manners. She hated guns. But of course she knew that men carried them for protection, especially in the West where the law wasn't yet fully defined or enforced.

"And a good thing he did," Meg said in a shivery but accurate assessment of their situation. She crossed her arms over her stomach and looked up at their savior with wide hazel eyes full of gratitude. "We thank you, sir."

Theodore Blane bent his head slightly in return and looked from Meg to Libby. His wide-set eyes were as blue as the morning sky. "You must be the young ladies Miz Primm's been expecting. I hear you come all the way from Boston."

A pleasing innocence showed in his face, and Libby was momentarily struck by the contrast between the gun and his lack of guile. When he pushed his broad-brimmed hat back on his head, a shock of copper hair strayed over a tanned forehead. He was no taller than she was. He wore a brown shirt, and a black neckerchief hung loosely at his throat. A fringed vest flapped open in the wind, and slightly bowed legs ended in boots with scuffed toes. He yanked off his hat and slapped it against his thigh. "Folks call me Teddy," he said with a shy grin.

It was strange to address people by their first names, but it was a custom Aunt Tillie had confessed to liking very much. Libby found herself adapting quickly. "I'm Elizabeth Carson," she said, then added, "Most people call me Libby, and this is my sister, Margaret."

"Meg," her sister corrected as she gave a customary curtsy, her flared skirt scraping the ground.

Libby followed suit as Teddy reached out to shake first Meg's hand and then hers. His hand was rough but warm and dry, his grip gentle but firm. "Yes, we're from Boston," she said, pleased to feel her heart resume its natural rhythm after the shock of the gunshot and the large dead snake. Her mind had been restored to its familiar curiosity.

"Pleased to know you both," Teddy said.

Libby looked back toward the house, wondering if the noise had sent anyone out to investigate. They were many yards away, but surely the gunshot had been heard. Yet no one stepped out onto the broad porch.

"Just an old rattler," Teddy said, following her gaze toward the house. "Ain't nothing new about gunshots in these parts. Between critters and target practice, the air's full of 'em."

She swallowed. "I see." They definitely were not in Boston anymore.

A beautiful mahogany roan ambled up to the fence, nickering softly, mane shining like obsidian. Teddy clapped a hand on its flank. "This is Queen, a right fine quarter horse. Miz Primm bought her at the auction in Lincoln County."

"She is beautiful," Libby said, reaching out to stroke the lovely white star on the animal's head. She was used to the horses that drew their carriages through streets and country lanes in Massachusetts, but it was quite a different thing to see the creatures running free and splendid with the sun gleaming on their powerful bodies.

"We have sidesaddles for the ladies. Would you like to ride her sometime? I mean, when you're not all dressed up like you are now." He blushed.

"Could we?" Libby asked eagerly.

"Sure. We have several that would give you a nice smooth ride. Queen here is a bit more lively than most."

"Is that so?" Libby said, and in that moment she decided that Queen would be her choice.

"Would you like to come in out of the sun?" Teddy asked. "I can show you the stable, the horse stalls and such." He paused, reddening slightly. "Got some clean bales you can rest on for a spell. Unless you'd rather go back to the house."

"No," Libby said quickly, eager to learn more about the life of a western cowboy without interference from Aunt Tillie. "But we don't want to keep you from your work. I suppose we've already distracted you."

Teddy shrugged. "I'm mostly done now. Been up since dawn."

He looked out onto the property. "Luke and Jeeter are riding fence today." Maybe he was thinking another hand would make a more suitable tour guide. "Hawk is herding the cattle in the south fork with the others." A shadow passed over his boyish face and quickly lifted. "But I'll be glad to show you around."

"That's very kind of you," Libby said, liking his friendly, easy manner. She'd heard that people in the West had hearts as wide as the prairie. "They'd give you the shirts off their backs," Aunt Tillie had said. And that was quite something, Libby thought, considering the intensity of the blistering sun that penetrated her shawl and dress at that moment.

They followed Teddy through the corral gate, passing a carriage with a leather top, an old buckboard with wooden wheels, and a long, slatted wagon loaded with something beneath a tarpaulin.

They entered the cool interior of the stable with its dozen or more empty stalls and walked into a recessed area with sacks, implements, and various supplies neatly stored. In one corner were a bedroll and a two-drawer chest. On top of it lay a sketchbook with a stick of charcoal angled across the open page. Tacked up on a rough-planked wall next to the chest were two black-and-white drawings.

Teddy took a low stool near the chest as Meg and Libby sat down on bales of straw. He pulled out a canteen and held it toward Libby. She took an eager draft, not allowing herself to consider its cleanliness or lack thereof, and handed the canteen to Meg.

"What exactly does a cowboy do?" Libby asked, wondering about the drawings but wanting to revive her flagging manners.

"Depends," Teddy said, stretching his legs out in front of him. "Sometimes we ride herd, round up strays, or brand 'em. And there are always fences that need fixing." He gave a little shrug. "Gotta curry the horses or muck out the stalls." He wrinkled his nose, sending the freckles dancing. "That ain't my favorite part, but Miz Primm's mighty particular."

"Have you been with my aunt very long?" Meg asked. There was a certain gleam in her hazel eyes, a look of admiration. It was clear that Meg liked this cowboy. Libby had learned to trust her sister's assessment of people. She was an excellent judge of character.

"Nope," he said. "Only a couple months. Come up north from Texas."

"Texas," Libby repeated. Much of the western lore she'd been hearing about involved that part of the country. "Are you a genuine cowboy then?" she asked.

Teddy grinned and ran a hand through his hair. "I suppose," he said shyly. "Mostly I handle horses. Cowpunching can be boring. It's long hours on the trail with sagebrush and horseflies. It's kind of lonely too." He shrugged, adding, "I like being with people."

Libby peered past him to appraise the sketches on the wall. One portrayed a fringed-jacketed cowboy on a bucking horse. The lines were good, the action captured in bold strokes. The other was a portrait of a young woman with long black hair threaded with beads and flowing over slender shoulders. The young Indian girl had dark eyes, solemn and fixed in an expression of sadness and patient endurance.

"Those are interesting pictures," Libby said hesitantly. "Are you an artist as well as a cowboy?"

His face reddened slightly but his eyes brightened. "I sketch some when I ain't working. It's something I do to pass the time now and again." He hitched up his shoulders and let them drop.

"I think they're very good indeed," Libby said, meaning it, and sorry to make her host uncomfortable. "I'm sure my aunt would think so too if she saw them."

"Yes, Mr. Blane," Meg put in, lapsing into the formal mode

of address she was accustomed to. "You are quite talented. May I ask where you studied art?"

He shook his head, laughing. "Shucks, Miss Meg. I ain't no mister, and I'm afraid I'm not much for studying. Spent my growing-up years going to school now and then when I wasn't helping my pa."

"Your father was a cowboy too?" Meg asked.

"No ma'am. Pa was a farmer, mostly cotton. Hard work. Like to broke his back, and it would have done me in too. But I was mustered with the Twenty-Fifth. Then, after the Indian War, I kept moving. Tried my hand at railroading and a few other things. Didn't like 'em much." He looked down at his hands, which Libby saw were red and chafed. "Miz Primm's good to work for, and I like being here." He paused and rubbed his jaw thoughtfully. "But I kinda like working over at the arena, you know, for the show."

Libby sat up straighter on the rough bale. "Do you mean the western show set up south of town? The one that famous Pony Express rider runs?"

"Buffalo Bill Cody himself," Teddy said, eyes lighting up. "He hired me on to work the show in the afternoons. You know, rope tricks and fancy riding and such." He cocked his head. "You know about the Wild West?"

"Not exactly," Libby said. "But last night on our way here from the train station, we passed a big area filled with tents and teepees and people coming and going. We saw horses and buffalo. It's quite a big settlement."

"I thought it might be a reservation," Meg said.

"The driver of our carriage told us it was where the performers from the show stay. We got out to take a closer look, and that's when we saw that poor man on the road." Libby frowned, remembering. "An Indian, and he was bleeding. We got him some water and tried to clean the wound. He must have hit his head." She swallowed. "We wanted to help. We couldn't leave him there."

Teddy narrowed his eyes and leaned forward. His face paled, and the patch of freckles stood out in bold relief.

"He was a quite a fearsome-looking Indian," Meg said. "He had a huge headdress of feathers, and beads around his neck." She plucked a piece of straw from the bale and twisted it between her fingers. "It was odd to see a crucifix hanging there amongst the beads."

Teddy let his breath out suddenly. "Is he all right?"

"We offered to drive him to his tent, but he seemed afraid or angry," Libby said. "It was clear he didn't trust us and wasn't going to let us help him. He got up and stalked off. He said, 'I walk.' And that's what he did."

"Our driver said he must have been part of the western show," Meg said.

Teddy ran a hand through his hair. He looked from Libby to Meg, his face knotted with worry. "That was not just any Indian. That was Sitting Bull." Teddy appeared to be waiting for a reaction. "He's the only one who wears a chieftain's headdress and a crucifix. He's a good friend of Buffalo Bill's and the real star of the show, even if he's hard to get along with sometimes. You sure he's all right?"

"We think so. As I said, he walked away." Libby was unnerved by Teddy's alarm. "Sitting Bull fought for the Sioux," she said, remembering her history.

"He only surrendered when all hope for a treaty was lost," Teddy added.

Could it be they had actually seen Sitting Bull, the great Sioux chief and warrior? Libby felt her pulse quicken.

Teddy leaned forward on the stool and rested his elbows on his knees. His eyes traveled to the sketch of the Indian girl. "She's his daughter and a friend." He was quiet for several seconds as he studied the sketch. Then he tore his eyes away and looked back at Libby and Meg. "There's been some trouble out at the arena, threats and accidents. The Colonel's worried that we might have to shut down the show."

Libby waited, unnerved by Teddy's alarm.

"Someone torched one of the teepees at night. Now Sitting Bull . . . ?" He raised both eyebrows and let out a long sigh. "The Colonel respects the Indians and supports their rights. Gives 'em a chance to earn their own money. He's brought quite a few from the reservation besides Sitting Bull. There's Walking Buffalo, Moccasin Tom, and Red Shirt. The Colonel fought them in the war but only because he had to. He says that every Indian outbreak he's ever known came from broken promises and broken treaties by the government."

Excitement rose with dread as Libby listened. Hadn't the white man done enough to wound and destroy these indigenous people? Now someone was harassing Cody's Wild West show. Was it because Indians were being included in the show? She bit her lip in frustration. "We'd like very much to see this Wild West show," Libby said, working to control her excitement.

"I can get you in," Teddy said importantly. "Sometimes we get free passes for our friends." He looked away shyly as though he had overstepped some social boundary. Aunt Tillie would definitely say he had, for they were of different social classes—well-bred society ladies and a simple cowboy from Texas. But they were in the West where the rules were still taking shape.

"Oh, will you take us?" Meg pleaded.

"Yes, please." Libby wanted to go immediately, but they already had social obligations. "We have to attend an event this afternoon, but perhaps another day?"

Teddy's face bloomed with pleasure. "I'll find out how

Sitting Bull is when I go to the arena this afternoon." He stopped and shook his head slowly. "It'll be mighty sad if he can't ride around on his big palomino." He gave Libby a probing look, and his voice grew husky. "You were kind to stop and help. A lot of folks wouldn't."

"I'm just glad he wasn't hurt worse," Libby said softly as she got up to leave.

Teddy extended an arm to usher them out of the barn.

At the stable door, a big man with a dark mustache appeared, carrying a saddle in one brawny arm. Easily twice Teddy's size, he flashed angry eyes first at Teddy and then at Libby and Meg.

Libby stiffened.

"So, Teddy Bear," the man growled, a sneer pulling the mustache down toward his prominent chin. "Thought you was s'posed to be mucking out them stalls, and here you are playing tea party with a couple of fancy ladies."

Teddy's mouth clamped shut. He shoved his fists into the pockets of his heavy work pants—perhaps, Libby thought, to keep from whacking the impudent interloper. He seemed more disgusted than intimidated. "Show some respect, Hawk," he said through gritted teeth. "These are Miz Primm's nieces."

The burly man with filthy britches and sweat rings on his shirt gave a mock bow. "Ladies," he said in short, punctuated syllables. "Ain't you a ways from the parlor out here with the stable boy?"

Aghast at such a display of knavery, Libby took a step toward the large, uncouth man. "Mr. Blane here was good enough to show us around the ranch," she said hotly. "And he defended us from a venomous snake that might have killed us."

Hawk threw his head back and laughed, showing dark, uneven teeth. "*Mister* Blane, is it? Ain't you the dandy?" he mocked, casting his dark gaze on Teddy. The offensive Hawk lumbered past them, his humorless laugh echoing as he went.

"I'm sorry," Teddy said. "He had no call to be so rude." He paused and lowered his head. "I hope you won't think badly of everyone here in Omaha. Ever since Hawk got let go at the Wild West, he's been riding me. He can be meaner than a snake when he's riled."

Meg smiled sweetly at Teddy and hastened to reassure him. "We thank you again for your kindness and your bravery," she said.

"We do indeed," Libby added evenly, though inside she was fuming over the burly man's treatment of Teddy Blane.

"If Miz Primm lets you go, I'll be pleased to escort you to the show at three o'clock tomorrow," Teddy said, brightening. "We may have to take the buckboard, unless Miz Primm lets us use the carriage." He gave them a conspiratorial smile and bowed in farewell.

5

Cabot Falls
Vermont, Present Day

Sofia felt her pace quicken as she approached the Cabot Falls Public Library, where the art show was to be held. Its spacious interior and beautifully carved woodwork never failed to inspire her. Built around the turn of the nineteenth century, it was initially funded through a generous bequest from a wealthy bibliophile. The building was impressive for its size alone, and its handsome gray brick and stained glass windows rivaled those of many churches.

The library was a perfect backdrop for works of the town's artists, Sofia decided. It would remain closed until the start of the show that evening, but there was a lot to do before the crowd arrived and before she had to go to the hotel to collect Howahkan, the guest artist. Julie and Marla, cochairs of the show with Sofia, had agreed to arrive by eight a.m. sharp to finish the preparations.

As Sofia approached the double glass doors, Marla strode purposefully across the marble floor to let her in. Besides being her good friend and fellow Pinot Painter, Marla was the head librarian and had been instrumental in the board's decision to allow the art show to be held within the library's hallowed walls.

"Good morning," Sofia greeted her. "Julie here yet?"

"She's on her way," Marla said, pushing back moist strands of blond hair that curved around her face like a pair of parentheses. She had rolled up the sleeves of her turquoise blouse and looked ready to tackle the day. She ran a tight ship, and she knew how to work with a sometimes-difficult library board too.

The scent of lemon polish mixed with the perennial smells of paper and leather lifted Sofia's spirits. It had been a difficult night. She'd done a fair amount of tossing and turning and waking from strange dreams. In one she was confronted by an angry Howahkan, a paintbrush in one hand and a tomahawk raised in the other. She sighed and tucked her purse underneath Marla's horseshoe desk.

"I heard that," Marla said, giving her a perceptive look. "Rough morning?"

Sofia shook her head and let out a long breath. Getting four kids off to school was often daunting, but this morning it had gone quite smoothly. It was the night before that had been rough. The hole in the quilt was small and, in the grand scheme of life, no huge disaster, but where had it come from? What had she done to cause it? Or not done to prevent it?

She talked it through with Marla, who always made her feel better, but it wasn't enough to erase the memory of the accusatory looks on her sisters' faces. The first part of Nonna's birthday celebration had been fun, but the hole in the quilt had ended the festivities. Rosa and Gina had gone home disgruntled, though they tried in some measure to cover up their feelings.

Sofia had been too tired and hurt to investigate the hole any further. She'd simply rewrapped the quilt in the cotton fabric and returned it to its trunk. Jim had told her not to worry, which was possible, at least for the moment, since he had taken her in his arms and reminded her how much he loved her.

Actually, it had been in a library that she had met Jim,

and it was his kindness that had drawn her to him. The college library that cradled her courting memories wasn't as grand as the edifice in Cabot Falls, but it would always be hallowed in her heart.

That long-ago day when she met her would-be husband, she had put in a grueling seven hours researching and writing an important essay that was due the next day. Her hair was a mess, her makeup nonexistent, and the bags under her eyes had bags. The room had been hot, and she was sweaty, disheveled, and hungry. She knew she must look like something the cat would refuse to drag in.

In walked Jim with his curly blond hair and deep blue eyes, wearing a crisp oxford shirt and looking like he'd stepped out of the barbershop. They knew each other but had done little more than say hello from time to time. Now he was headed for her table, carrying a brown paper bag and a weathered briefcase.

"Don't you ever take a break?" he'd asked, dropping down next to her at the table. "You've been here all day. You must be really tired."

How had he known? Had she been so engrossed, so over-whelmed, that she'd not noticed him? He had such a look of compassion in his blue eyes that she felt a lump in her throat. She had actually wanted to cry. She was tired, stressed, and certain that her paper was destined for disaster. She hadn't been able to say a word.

It was very late in the afternoon, and they were alone in a secluded corner of the library. Quietly he drew a chocolate cream doughnut from the bag and gave her a wink. "I thought you could use some fortification." He'd handed it to her on a paper napkin and smiled, making tiny creases around his eyes.

That was the beginning. She fell in love with his perceptive mind, his kind heart, and his ready helpfulness. Eighteen years and four kids later, she was still struck by his outright goodness. A woman with such a man could endure anything, couldn't she?

"Ah, there's Julie," Marla said, interrupting Sofia's pleasant memory and going to unlock the door.

Now they would set their minds and energies on final preparations for the art show. Thirty entries, framed and priced, had been accepted from local artists who welcomed the chance to show their work, possibly even land a sale. They had already placed most of the art on beautifully polished shelves that lined the walls. Of course there would be a special area for Howahkan's paintings, and displaying them was their task for this morning.

"Did the shipment come from New York?" Julie asked breathlessly, speeding toward Sofia with Marla trailing behind. She carried a garment bag, likely holding good clothes to change into when it was time for the show. Sofia had left hers in the car until it was time to pick up Howahkan at the hotel.

Julie flung off a light jacket, revealing a sleeveless emerald shell. Excitement bubbled in her green eyes, and her red hair seemed even more electric than usual as it spilled around her face and onto her shoulders in long, springy curls. "Where is it?"

"You mean *them*," Marla said. "There are at least two dozen crates. Our guest artist's agent doesn't do things by halves."

Sofia sighed at the mention of Howahkan's agent, with whom she had endured considerable correspondence. They hadn't met in person, but if anyone was more disagreeable than the silent Howahkan, it was Mr. Rathbone Steele. How could someone so urbane and sophisticated do business in such a rigid and obnoxious manner? He wasn't willing to give an inch by way of accommodation, and he expected his orders to be carried out.

He couldn't possibly get the artwork to Cabot Falls until the day before the show, meaning a last-minute scramble for Sofia and her team. Volunteers had helped to arrange and document the local entries, and they had done a really excellent job, but Sofia and her two friends would have just a few hours to display each of Howahkan's works in time for the Thursday evening opening of the show, which was scheduled to run through Saturday afternoon.

"I brought tin snips in case the crates are wired," Julie said as the three of them went to the locked room at the south end of the library where the art had been stored overnight. "I'm not about to break my nails trying to open them." She had painted sunsets on her fingernails in honor of their Native American guest artist.

Marla and Sofia exchanged knowing looks. Julie's nails were as wild as her art and were legendary in Cabot Fall, works of art in themselves.

"They're gorgeous!" Sofia said.

"Amazing," concurred Marla. But she was concentrating on the crates and began drawing out their contents. Most yielded a single painting, carefully wrapped in an acid-free carton to avoid UV infiltration.

"Better read Rathbone Steele's instructions or else his *wrath* will be on our *bones*," Sofia said. She brought the file from the horseshoe desk, and the three of them sat down to review the brochures before beginning to place the art.

"'Skylar Blane is his given name, but the artist is known by the single Native American moniker, Howahkan,'" Marla read aloud from his bio.

"He's handsome," Julie said, pointing to the photo. "Look at that face. It looks like he's been carved out of marble. And have you ever seen hair that long on a man?"

The shiny black hair in the photo cascaded over his left shoulder in small, even waves, as though it had been braided and released. He wore a black dress shirt, a long beaded necklace, and a suede vest. At the airport he had been wearing a modern charcoal suit with a burgundy tie and shiny patent leather shoes. The mix of two cultures had a jarring effect.

Sofia studied the photo, recalling the inscrutable man she had encountered and tried to engage.

"You met him," Julie said. "Tell me what he's like."

"Yes, I met him," Sofia said, nodding. She stared down at the photo and drew in a long breath.

"That doesn't sound good," Marla said.

Sofia shrugged and read from the brochure. "Howahkan means 'of the mysterious voice' or 'the mysterious voice,'" she mumbled. "Mysterious I get, but voice? I wouldn't know about that part."

Julie frowned and flipped a stray curl off her face. "Why's that?"

"Because he hardly said two words to me on our trip from the airport to the hotel. Either he has no voice, mysterious or otherwise, or my conversational skills are to blame."

"Hardly that," Julie said, still frowning. "But I've read that he's something of a loner. Well, aren't all Native Americans the strong, silent type?"

"That," Marla said with more than a touch of disdain, "is a stereotype foisted on a population whose voices have largely been silenced."

Julie nodded, chastened. "Yeah, I get that. I guess we all know about the long Trail of Tears."

"It was more than one trail," Sofia added, "and more tears than we can ever imagine. I doubt that we'll ever make up for everything stolen from them in the name of progress." She continued to pore over the details in the brochure. "It says here that Howahkan is the great-grandson of a marginally known sketch artist from the late 1800s, a cowboy who married a Sioux Indian girl. He paints from those charcoal sketches of his great-grandfather's," Sofia said. "Such fabulous western scenes."

"Did he say anything at all?" Julie asked.

Sofia relayed the events of the day before from the moment the artist had stepped toward her near the luggage carousel. She had been holding a placard with Cabot Falls Art Show printed on it, but there was no need to confirm his identity. "Mr. Blane?" she had mumbled, taken aback by the imposing figure in a three-piece suit and white shirt. Across his chest, a beaded necklace with a silver medallion glistened. "Skylar Blane?"

"Howahkan," he said, just the single word. His name. He had frowned and taken the hand she held out in greeting but quickly released it. His hand was long and slender, almost delicate, allowing only the briefest pressure in hers. She had introduced herself, and they had walked in silence to her car. After they were out on the open stretch of road, she'd asked if he'd had a pleasant journey. If he'd heard her, he gave no indication. He'd simply looked through the windshield, sitting arrow-straight in the seat.

A quarter of an hour passed before she'd tried again. "We're looking forward to your visit with us. I understand you attended art school in Manhattan." He hadn't answered but had turned to look at her with an expression of infinite sadness. Unnerved, she'd returned her eyes to the road.

"He didn't talk at all," Sofia said to her friends, "and he looked so sad." She shook her head. "I can't imagine how we'll get through this show. He's as silent as a tomb."

Marla looked pensive. "I have heard the rumor about him being a loner." She paused before adding in a quiet voice, "I didn't know he suffered from depression."

Rathbone Steele had certainly not prepared them for the silent, inscrutable Howahkan. Sofia and the others hadn't investigated him very closely either, she realized now. They had simply been captivated by his work.

A gasp escaped Marla's lips as she unsheathed a painting. Sofia and Julie followed her gaze to a canvas depicting a sagebrush plain on which buffalo grazed. The backdrop was a beautiful series of turquoise and purple mountain peaks, their tops glistening against a lavender sky. The luminous colors sent a tremor through Sofia. At first she didn't see the subtle outline of an American Indian in the lower left foreground, looking into the scene. It was the man's back that the viewer saw, but somehow the lines evoked an almost palpable pain.

"He's really good," Julie breathed. "I'd love to have it, but the price will probably be out of sight."

Sofia read the selling price on the attached card. It was high but not exorbitant.

"Look at this one." Marla lifted a smaller canvas from its wrapping and held it away from her for a better view. "This is Sitting Bull, the great Sioux chief." Standing with the stone-faced chief in full headdress was a young Caucasian girl dressed in a demure knee-length skirt and loose blouse, chestnut hair flowing over her narrow shoulders. Marla read the card with the painting's description. "'Sitting Bull with his adopted daughter.'"

"It's absolutely charming," Julie declared, but her praise was interrupted by an insistent knock at the library's front door.

"It's only ten thirty," Marla said. "I hope people aren't going to start gathering early."

Sofia saw it was Ryan Quimby and another officer from the Cabot Falls Police Department at the door. Had they been dispatched to monitor the community gathering, to make sure everything was in order? There was no good reason for the sudden sense of foreboding that made her catch her breath.

Sofia liked Ryan, with his broad smile and boyish freckles. He'd grown up in Cabot Falls and now, at thirty, his training behind him, he had returned to the town he so clearly loved. He was studying for a forensics degree and took his job seriously.

There was a somber look on Officer Quimby's face as he walked toward the desk where a poster on a tall easel announced the art show. He stopped in front of it, studied it quietly, and then turned to Sofia. "I'm afraid your guest artist won't be appearing tonight."

The three of them stared at him in silence.

Sofia felt her stomach do a flip.

"When the maid went to his room this morning, she found him." Officer Quimby's face seemed to pale, making the freckles across his nose stand out. "I'm afraid Mr. Blane is dead."

6

Omaha, Nebraska
June 1885

Libby smoothed the folds of her mauve silk dress and, after a satisfactory glance into the mirror, felt ready to join Aunt Tillie in the parlor. Carriages and horses had been arriving over the last half hour, but she and Meg had been told to delay coming to the tea so that a proper "entrance" could be made.

"But can we not help in the entertaining?" Libby had asked earlier in the day. "Surely there is much to be done."

"Certainly not," Aunt Tillie had said forcefully. "Greta has everything in hand, and you, my darlings, are my guests. I intend to show you off as the refined young ladies you are."

So they had taken time with their dresses, their hair and jewelry, all the while discussing their experiences with Teddy, the coiled snake, the Wild West show, and the American Indian named Sitting Bull.

"It will be so exciting to see Buffalo Bill at the arena," Libby said as she prepared to enter the bustling parlor.

"Yes," Meg agreed. "But today we must do our best to make Aunt Tillie happy."

"Of course, sister," Libby said. She was not surprised that her aunt had brought to the prairie fine furnishings from her former home. Some pieces had been purchased in Omaha, but all were designed in the best styles of the era, including solid tables and an assortment of ebonized and cane-bottom chairs.

A sofa and overstuffed chairs were arranged around a carved-stone fireplace of stunning detail. It featured a circle of bees on the center arch and stylized chrysanthemums and birds on each side. On the left, a large Japanese egret was carved into the stone.

Libby could almost imagine herself back in a Boston parlor as she viewed the sturdy, attractive window hangings. They were drawn back to allow the sun's rays to brighten the heavy damask wall coverings and dark polished furnishings. A carpet of plain brown felt bordered with green matched the embroidered lambrequin that adorned the mantel.

Tillie sat on a chintz-covered sofa, drinking tea from one of her fine china cups. Libby couldn't help admiring her aunt's uncorseted tea gown of soft gray satin that complemented her silver-threaded hair. The formfitting bodice of her dress featured a scalloped neckline. Like the other women, she wore little jewelry, the custom perhaps for afternoon wear in the West.

The fad of hoop skirts had ended, replaced by bustles that allowed for freer movement. *Thank goodness*, Libby thought. But even freer yet must have been the clothing that allowed pioneers to work hard in the blazing sun and forbidding soil without thought to fashion—clothing like Greta wore, or likely Aunt Tillie had probably worn when she and Hector were developing their land.

Tillie was chatting amiably with two ladies seated in black wickerwork chairs. One had a figure like a pouter pigeon and wore a hat with an enormous plume that wiggled when she talked. The feather came precariously close to a dour-faced woman in a black bombazine dress who seemed to be holding forth on a topic that clearly excited her.

Greta set a tray filled with delicate pastries on a carved sideboard and retreated as Libby stepped into the circle of guests with Meg following close behind. Aunt Tillie's handsome face beamed as she caught Libby's eye, and she set her teacup down on a low table. Her voice rang through the conversation as she rose and addressed the ladies in the circle. "I'm so pleased to present to you my nieces, Elizabeth and Margaret Carson, newly arrived from Boston." She swept an arm out to include the two men near the fireplace in her introduction.

Libby glanced toward the two, who were absorbed in agitated conversation. Possibly it was a political discussion or a disagreement over business. Clearly they were not in accord, whatever the issue. The taller and younger of the men was sandy haired and wore a well-cut dove-gray suit. He had his back to Libby, but she could see his hands clench and unclench at his sides as he pressed in toward his companion.

The older man, balding and stout, was a good four inches shorter. The hair that escaped the top of his head had clustered in mutton chops on his florid cheeks. He wore a knee-length frock coat over his prominent stomach and stood on small feet that turned slightly outward, reminding Libby of an overfed duck.

Libby blushed at her uncomplimentary metaphor and turned her attention to the ladies, who did not rise but gave little nods and murmurs of greeting. They inspected their young visitors with as much interest as could be camouflaged by good breeding.

"Join us, my dears," Aunt Tillie said, gesturing to the chairs across from the women. She poured tea into china cups painted with tiny roses and handed them to Libby and Meg. "My nieces have completed their terms at one of the finest finishing schools in Boston," she trilled. "And now they've come to spend their summer holiday with me."

"How delightful," said the pouter pigeon, whom Tillie addressed as Miss Lily Penfield. "You'll find we have some excellent social gatherings here in Omaha. And goodness knows we need the influence of fine young ladies such as yourselves."

"We do indeed," said the sharp-nosed taller woman dressed in black. *A modified mourning dress*, Libby surmised. She knew that American women didn't adhere to the darker conventions of Great Britain but still observed a period of mourning, including the wearing of black. *At least*, thought Libby, *it isn't trimmed with stiff, scratchy crepe.*

"This is Miss Harriet Goodwin," Tillie said sympathetically. "She's recently been bereaved of her dear Aunt Cornelia, God rest her soul."

Miss Goodwin seemed to ignore the comment. "Our young women need good role models," she said, dark eyes suddenly passionate. "Women who know how to act with good breeding and polite manners, unlike some of those loose women who flaunt themselves on the stage. Some of them even ride horses like men and sport guns."

Lily Penfield gave a small shake of her feathered hat and cleared her throat. Tillie smiled nervously and asked if she might pour more tea. But Miss Goodwin hadn't finished. Leaning closer to Libby, she said, "Fine young women such as yourselves wouldn't bother with bawdy shows such as the one that Indian scout Cody puts on over at the arena."

"Oh, have you seen it?" Meg asked innocently.

"Certainly not!" Two bright spots appeared on Miss Goodwin's sallow cheeks. She gave her head a toss, nearly dislodging her hat, and sniffed contemptuously.

Libby took a deliberate sip of tea and peered over the rim of her cup. Teddy had told her that some Nebraskans were quite interested in Colonel Cody's show; indeed, they were flocking to watch the reenactments of Indian wars and the exploits of cowboys and trick shooters. Were there women in the Wild West show too? And were they "bawdy"?

"We are doing our best to tame the unhealthy appetites of

the populace here. We've a majority male population, of course, due to Omaha's rail boom," Miss Goodwin said. "Sadly, this led to the development of bars and gambling houses and other such uncivilized pursuits." She waved a hand dismissively. "Tell me, Miss Carson, are you familiar with the work of Miss Frances Willard?" She raised a dark brow that seemed too heavy for her narrow face.

Libby nodded, but her attention was diverted when she noticed that the taller of the men near the fireplace was looking rather steadily in her direction. He stood very erect, a studied expression in his eyes' greenish-blue color that she found magnetic and at the same time disturbing. His light brown hair glinted amber in the ray of sun slanting across it.

He looks to be in his early thirties, she thought. *And likely married.* She wondered briefly which of the ladies in the parlor might be his wife, and if she knew how intensely he was looking at a strange woman at this moment.

Miss Goodwin cocked her head, obviously waiting for an answer. Libby knew something about the national leader of the temperance union who had been born in New York but educated in Illinois. Frances Willard had helped found the Evanston Ladies' College in 1869 and later became its president.

Apparently, Harriet Goodwin decided to answer her own question. "She has quite distinguished herself as the president of the Women's Christian Temperance Movement," she continued, "and always with the noblest of female graces."

"I do think that's so important," said Lily Penfield, "don't you?"

Libby nodded again, feeling stifled. She very much would have liked to escape the company of Harriet Goodwin and Lily Penfield, but good manners forbade it. Perhaps Meg needed more tea—but her sister was chatting amiably with a middle-aged, cherubic-faced woman who had quietly taken a place in the cluster of chairs.

Aunt Tillie glanced somewhat warily toward the disputing men at the fireplace and came to her rescue. "Libby, dear, I want you to meet our mayor and his nephew." Taking her by the hand, she whisked her away from the circle of ladies. "He's quite unattached, by the way," she added in Libby's ear as they crossed the room toward the fireplace. "Young Mr. Ealy."

Libby studied the scene as he took a biscuit from the Wedgwood tray Sonja held toward him, unaware of her scrutiny. Libby thought she saw a look of disdain interrupt the young servant girl's usually placid Scandinavian features as she waited with the tray in her hand. *A maid looking down on the gentry?* But it had only been a fleeting glance and probably meant nothing.

When they reached the men standing near the fireplace, Tillie said in her animated soprano, "I'm pleased to introduce Mayor Augustus Quaid." She gave Libby a slight push forward, adding, "Mayor, this is my niece, Miss Elizabeth Carson of Boston."

Will she never tire of making the Boston connection as though it were some sort of merit badge? Libby curtsied, endeavoring as she did so to keep her eyes on the mayor rather than on the commanding figure next to him.

"My dear Mrs. Primm," said the older man, stepping forward on his small turned-out feet and bowing from his portly waist. "How kind of you to host this excellent reception." His mutton chops rose and fell as he spoke.

"In your honor, Mayor," Tillie said, coloring. She turned to Libby. "Mayor Quaid has done a great deal for our city, providing for fire prevention and water delivery services, not to mention grading our streets, which were once a frightful mess."

Not waiting for a humble acknowledgment of the accolade, Tillie looked up at the tall young man with green-blue eyes. "And this is his nephew, Mr. Robert Ealy. Robert, my niece, Miss Elizabeth Carson."

Libby curtsied, aware of a slight fluttering in her stomach. He was handsome in his gray suit and pale blue cravat. In its silky center was a pin with an unusual stone that caught the sunrays beaming through the glass windows. From his elegant head to his polished black shoes, every inch spoke of gentility. *Unattached,* Aunt Tillie had said. *Why is he not yet married?*

"I'll leave you, dear," Tillie said patting her arm. "I must see to Duchess. She was groaning something awful in the night. I think she'll have her puppies today, hopefully not until after the tea. I'll go encourage her a little." With that she was gone, and when Libby looked up after a few reasonable seconds with eyes politely downcast, she saw that the mayor, too, had gone to join other circles, leaving her standing alone with Robert Ealy.

"Pleased to meet you, Miss Carson," he said, his voice deep and slightly raspy, as though he might have been recovering from a cold. "I understand you and your sister are having a holiday here in Omaha." The puzzling eyes resembled glacial ice, but when he suddenly smiled, they turned a lustrous cerulean blue.

"We only arrived yesterday, but it's been a most satisfying journey so far," she said. "My sister and I are grateful to see this exciting country."

"I hope you'll allow me to show you some of our more interesting sights." At her shocked expression, his face softened. "I apologize if I seem forward. Here in the West we don't have time to stand on ceremony. Things are changing all the time." A twinkle lit the blue-green gaze. "Someone might shoot our legs from under us if we wait too long."

She gazed at him in surprise. They had only just been introduced. Show her around, indeed! Then he gave a throaty chuckle.

"Forgive me?" he asked with a pleading tilt of his tawny head. "I mean no disrespect. I am offering, with your aunt's permission and your charming sister's company as well, to show you our fair city at a time convenient to you."

She struggled for coherent speech, and a small laugh escaped her lips.

"Good," came the quick response as though she had agreed to accompany him in so many words. "For now, maybe you'll join me for a breath of air on your aunt's handsome porch. I assure you, we'll be well chaperoned."

"You mock me, sir," she managed.

"Certainly not. I merely need an escape from the heat and noise in this room." He gave her a conspiratorial grin. "And you might need a respite from the venerable Miss Goodwin."

Unable to suppress a smile, she walked with him through the exit leading to the broad stone porch with its wide-armed wicker chairs. He waited for her to sit, then dropped down across from her. Sheltered from the afternoon sun, Libby breathed in air fragrant with alfalfa. It was definitely much to be preferred over the cloying atmosphere in the parlor. Several guests were also taking the air, ambling along the winding driveway bordered by tall grasses that swayed in the breeze.

"And have you found Omaha to your liking, Miss Carson?" Robert asked.

"Indeed," Libby said. "I had no idea the prairie was so vast and so beautiful." She paused, noting the smooth, angled plane of his face. Most men wore mustaches, sideburns, or beards, but Robert was clean-shaven, making him look younger than the tiny lines at his eyes would suggest. "Have you been in Nebraska long?"

"Not long," he said. "My uncle needed a hand with his banking business here, so I headed west after the Plains Wars ended." He paused and peered off into the distance through narrowed eyes as though regarding something disturbing or unpleasant. A long moment passed in silence.

"War is terrible," Libby said quietly, assuming that scenes of battle had sobered his mood. Her own cousins, with whom she'd grown up in Massachusetts, had gone to war and never returned. So many had died, leaving behind bereaved families and communities, destroying native peoples and livelihoods. She read the agony of war in Robert's face and was saddened.

He remained still for several seconds more; then, in a low voice, he said, "My brother, James, was only seventeen when he was killed by those red devils!" Anger hardened his features for a second or two, and then he lifted his chin suddenly and straightened his tie as if to recover his equilibrium. The ice-blue eyes warmed to green. "But let's not speak of war on such a beautiful afternoon. Tell me about your trip and what you plan to do with your holiday."

"My sister and I had a most entertaining ride from the train," she began. "After the long hours of sitting and the press of so many people, the lovely prairie was a welcome change." She thought she might tell him about finding the wounded Indian, Sitting Bull, but the way he'd spoken of the Plains War stopped her.

Red devils. Robert Ealy probably wasn't alone in his assessment of the Indians who, in their fight to preserve their way of life, had battled with the pioneer settlers. She was eager to lighten the conversation. "We've heard so much about the West, my sister and I. We couldn't wait to see it for ourselves." She hesitated before adding, "We're hoping to go to Buffalo Bill's Wild West show while we're here."

A cloud passed over Robert's face like a sudden summer storm. "They're a bunch of ruffians, and Cody is the worst of them, glorifying all those Indians. Haven't we suffered enough at the hands of the red man?"

Stunned by his outburst, Libby could think of nothing to say. But as suddenly as his anger had come, it was gone. "Never mind, my dear Miss Carson," he said more quietly. "I can show you much more delightful entertainments than Cody's circus can provide." He smiled, looking deeply into her eyes. "Something worthy of a refined young lady like you."

Libby folded her hands together to calm herself. Were all the men in the West so quick with their assessments, so free with their compliments? This strange man, so obviously well connected and available, had freely shown his admiration, stirring up conflicting emotions in her.

Everything happened very fast in this wild, wonderful country. It was enough to make a girl's head spin, and she prided herself on keeping her head and heart under control.

But she was aware that under Robert Ealy's scrutiny, her cheeks were hot. Yet at the same time, a shiver went through her.

7

Cabot Falls, Vermont
Present Day

On Friday morning, Sofia waited in the small reading room of the library for the other members of the art show committee. She stared blankly at the notebook where minutes of their meetings were kept in carefully divided sections. Around her, Howahkan's paintings were just as they had left them the day before. Her heart was heavy as stone. A promising young artist was dead. An event that was supposed to bring culture and enjoyment to the community was now postponed, perhaps indefinitely.

After she'd found out about Howahkan's death the previous day, Sofia had gone home and waited for Jim. She had planned to be away at the art show all day and most of the evening, leaving her husband to feed the kids and get them to their clubs and sporting events. When Jim had entered the kitchen, she'd thrown her arms around his neck.

Sofia wasn't given to emotional outbursts, but the tears had flowed freely as she clung to him. "Oh, Jim!" When she had regained control, he had gently pulled away and searched her face. She had poured out the awful news of Howahkan's death—how Officer Ryan Quimby had come directly to the library with the dreadful news, and how she had likely been the last person to see the young artist alive.

They had hastily prepared posters informing the public that the art show would not open Thursday as originally planned. *Postponed until further notice due to unforeseen circumstances.* They informed everyone that the library would be open for regular use in the morning, but the reading room where the Native American artist's paintings were to be displayed would be closed.

"We need to know who to contact," Officer Quimby had said. "For . . . identification purposes."

Ryan had the necessary fortitude to keep law and order in Cabot Falls, but he was a sensitive man. Sofia knew he was trying to temper harsher language. Someone had to identify the body.

She had given him the contact information for Rathbone Steele, Howahkan's agent. But surely there was someone else in his life. How would his family take the news? Who would mourn this suddenly extinguished flame?

She had learned that large amounts of a tricyclic antidepressant had been found in Howahkan's system and that he had left a note reading simply, *I can't do this anymore. I am sorry.* He had overdosed on his prescription medicine, apparently on purpose, judging by the suicide note that was handwritten on his personal stationery.

Now, facing Marla and Julie around a small table in the library's reading room, Sofia shook her head. "I can't believe it. I knew something was wrong when I met him at the airport. He was so obviously troubled. I wish I would have said something, done something."

"What could you do?" Marla said firmly. "You had no way of knowing."

"Of course not," Julie added, grasping Sofia's arm in complete solidarity. "You said yourself that he didn't even talk to you." She shook her wild mane of red hair and drummed her fingernails on the table. "So what are we going to do now about the show?"

"I guess we could go ahead and have it with our local artists. We could avoid even mentioning him." As Marla spoke, she shook her head slowly in a dismissive gesture. "The rumor mill will be turning at a furious rate. The news is likely all over town right now."

Sofia nodded. Her friend Marla was no stranger to sudden death. Ten years earlier, Marla's husband had died suddenly of a rare heart condition, leaving Marla to raise their son, Tim, now fifteen. Still in her forties, she had only recently begun to date again. Sofia continued to hope that Marla would find someone worthy of her.

Julie, a public relations specialist, seldom minced words. "We'll have to pack up all those paintings and send them back to New York," she said grimly. "All that work for nothing. Shame too . . . they're really good."

Sofia took a deep breath. "Well, we can't do anything right away. We have to wait for the rest of the committee. They have a right to know what has happened and to offer their suggestions." Connie Hamilton, who had called to say she would be late, would have some good input. A local real estate vendor and watercolorist, Connie was a strong supporter of the arts along with her wealthy husband, who owned a small chain of auto supply stores.

Then Sofia groaned inwardly, thinking of Homer Winslow. He would be considerably less helpful, especially since he had been against inviting the Native American artist in the first place. "With all the local talent we have right here, why do we need an outsider coming in?" he had grumbled. "Why let some Indian hopeful cut into our sales?"

Marla had shot back a rapid-fire rebuke. "'Some Indian'? I can't believe you're so small-minded and bigoted."

But of course, they could believe it. Homer had endeared himself to few in Cabot Falls and was something of a boor with his nearly comical affected manner. In addition, he had delusions of grandeur, as did his mother, who had named her son after Winslow Homer, the famous nineteenth-century American seascape artist. Homer Winslow's paintings were pleasant enough but predictable and poor imitations of his namesake's work.

"Speak of the devil," Julie muttered under her breath.

Homer Winslow walked briskly toward them on small feet. He was little more than five feet four inches and portly, in a dark suit jacket buttoned tightly across his chest.

"Well, ladies, we have a situation on our hands," he said with a glint of satisfaction in his button-like eyes. Homer swept a stubby arm around the reading room where Howahkan's paintings were arranged. The images included an old cowboy on a graying horse, a young Indian maiden kneeling near a water trough, and Sitting Bull in a full Sioux headdress, standing with a young white girl.

Homer's chin, with its round little dimple, jutted forward in a pouting expression. "I told you we shouldn't bring in that outsider," he said.

Sofia had an urge to laugh, but at the same time she felt sorry for him. At forty-plus years old and living with his mother, he was often the butt of jokes. He had to be lonely and frustrated, working as a clerk in his mother's upscale gift shop and spending his leisure hours painting mediocre seascapes.

Homer stabbed a finger on a stack of brochures that carried Howahkan's photo and uttered a disdainful grunt. "Those Indians never could hold their liquor," he spouted with a truculent glare. "Now he's gone and offed himself and left us in the lurch, upsetting the whole town. Besides, who could trust a man with a barrette in his hair?"

"Homer Winslow," Julie snapped, "you have a mean mouth and an empty head. What in the world is wrong with you?"

Sofia saw that Marla was angry too and ready to explode, but Winifred Winslow was the chairperson of the library board, and offending her little boy could jeopardize Marla's job. "Let's calm down and talk about this like mature adults," Sofia said. She glared at Homer and pointed to an empty chair at the table. "Sit down," she ordered, adding "please" and drawing a deep breath.

But Homer wasn't finished. "I say we open the show as a Cabot Falls event, pure and simple. No phony outsiders." He shook his round head and swished a white handkerchief across his perspiring forehead. The gesture was theatrical, comical. One had to laugh at Homer—or cry.

Connie's apologetic entrance gave Sofia a chance to de-escalate the conflict in the room. She cleared her throat. "The truth of the matter is that we have a contract that involves not only the artist, but his agent, who, by the way, is due to arrive in Cabot Falls very shortly."

Rathbone Steele, of course, had been notified immediately that the artist was dead, and he had confirmed that he would be coming to their town immediately. He'd made it clear that under no circumstances were they to show Howahkan's paintings until he arrived.

"We don't want to make things worse, so let's not make any hasty decisions," Sofia said. How things could get any worse, however, she couldn't imagine. "Our patrons will understand the necessity to delay the show. The important thing in all of this is that a man is dead, and we don't yet know the cause for certain." She stared directly at Homer as she continued.

"His family hasn't been located, and arrangements have to be made." She felt her throat constrict as she recalled the troubled face of the guest artist. A life had been lost. How could they carry on with business as usual? Whatever the cause, Howahkan's death was a tragedy of profound proportions.

Any man's death diminishes me, because I am involved in mankind. John Donne's classic line from the poem "No Man Is an Island" rang in her mind.

By force of will, Sofia controlled her shaky voice and called the meeting to order, something she had been dreading. What could they do until more information was available? She cleared her throat to address the situation, but she was suddenly interrupted by a knock on the reading room door. Marla rose to answer it.

Officer Quimby, looking robust and official in his police blues, quietly surveyed the small group around the table.

"Officer Quimby," Sofia greeted him, curious and at the same time greatly relieved at the interruption. Had the coroner ruled on a cause of death? Were they about to hear the dreaded word *suicide*? She cleared her throat. "We were getting ready to discuss what to do about the art show. Do you have any information for us?"

"It's an open investigation at this point," he said in serious, if not grim, response. Once more, his penetrating eyes traveled around the table, taking each person's measure. "We need to get a statement from each of you." He glanced somewhat apologetically at Sofia. "We took yours last night, Mrs. Parker, but I need to know where the rest of you were at the time of the incident, Wednesday night."

No one said anything right away as they tried to absorb what the officer's words meant. The police knew a medication overdose had killed Howahkan, and they had a suicide note with the artist's chilling last words. So why were they being questioned about their whereabouts at the time Howahkan had supposedly died?

Sofia felt the tension in the room.

"Just routine," the policeman said, trying a smile. "Let's start with you, Ms. Dixon. I believe you're the head librarian here?" It was a fact he knew, of course, but this was an official investigation after all.

"Yes," Marla said quietly. "I was here until seven thirty Wednesday night with a number of volunteers. I'd be glad to give you their names. At eight o'clock, Peter Grebel picked me up at home." She glanced at Sofia and Julie with some embarrassment, for she hadn't shared this with her friends. "We went out to dinner at the Stone Eagle. We left at nine thirty, and Peter brought me home."

Julie crossed her arms over her forest-green suit. It might have been construed as a defiant gesture if one didn't know Julie. "I left the library at six and went home," she said firmly. "I helped the girls with their homework, and after that Mark and I watched the ten o'clock news together." She swept her vibrant fingernails through her mass of red hair and then fixed her green eyes on Officer Quimby.

"And you, Mrs. Hamilton?" Officer Quimby probed, turning to Connie.

"I was showing the Grenville house to prospective buyers from Virginia. I was tied up with them until nearly ten o'clock. Their names are—"

"Thank you," Officer Quimby said, apparently satisfied without names being supplied.

"I don't understand what this is all about," Homer broke in, dark eyes flashing in his flushed face. "Why the third degree?" He brandished the white handkerchief again and wiped his forehead, looking like he might be ill.

"It's routine, Mr. Winslow," Officer Quimby said, turning his steady gaze on the little man. "How about you? Where were you Wednesday night?"

He wiped his forehead again. "I closed the gift shop at five thirty and went home like I do almost every night. You can ask Mother."

"Is that so?" Officer Quimby said, considering his hapless quarry with a steady gaze. "Maybe it would be best if we continue this down at the station, Mr. Winslow."

Homer stood up, nearly overturning a glass of water at his place. "Why? What is this all about? I don't have to go anywhere."

"Come now, Mr. Winslow. Let's make this easy on everyone."

"I don't have anything to hide!" Homer half shouted. "I'm a citizen of this town, and I don't appreciate being manhandled."

"No one is manhandling you," Officer Quimby said with what Sofia could see was forced control. "A man is dead, and we have reason to believe that Mr. Blane wasn't alone in his hotel room. Furthermore, Mr. Winslow, we have an eyewitness who saw you in the hotel lobby on Wednesday night."

Winslow's face turned from red to white in startled seconds. "That's impossible. I told you I was at home." He glanced helplessly at Julie and Sofia.

"If you weren't there, we need to clear that up," Officer Quimby said.

Sofia felt her stomach lurch. Something was tugging at the back of her mind. What was it Homer had said earlier? *Who could trust a man with a barrette in his hair?*

When she'd driven Howahkan to the hotel, she had seen the gold clip he was wearing to secure his heavy hair. It could be thought of as a barrette, she supposed. But all the promotional photos showed him with his hair loose. How could Homer Winslow know he wore it clipped back unless he had seen him that night?

Was it possible that his disdain for the guest artist had led him to do something stupid or criminal? Was it possible that Howahkan had been murdered?

8

Omaha, Nebraska
June 1885

Teddy hopped down from the carriage with a broad grin. He was dressed much as he had been the first day Libby had met him—in a fawn-colored shirt, close-fitting trousers of some heavy fabric, and boots that rode high on his calves. A blue print scarf at his neck flapped in the breeze as he tipped his broad-brimmed hat. Libby saw several of the ranch hands moving about, but there was no sign of the bully who had harassed him in the stable.

Teddy was a thoughtful, artistic sort, an odd mix of visionary and cowboy. She hoped the other hired staff were less uncouth than the obnoxious Hawk and treated him with the kindness he deserved. Maybe someday people would realize how talented he was too.

Aunt Tillie had given Meg and Libby permission to go to the Wild West show with Teddy. She had also agreed to let them use the handsome carriage drawn by her two prized harness horses. Teddy's horse was tied behind and stood patiently, switching his black tail to ward off the menacing blackflies. It was the horse he would ride in the arena with the other cowboys, though he admitted to working largely behind the scenes.

A bunch of ruffians, and Cody is the worst of them. That had been Robert Ealy's assessment. Harriet Goodwin would likewise find it unfitting for young ladies of fine breeding. As for Aunt Tillie, she was cautious and ambivalent but had nonetheless given in to their pleas to see a real western show.

"Mind you stick close to Teddy, and don't go wandering off," she had warned, waggling a finger in their eager faces. "Your mother will throttle me if I let anything happen to you. I'd go along if it weren't for Duchess. She's much agitated and ready to drop her puppies." Then she had pulled her nieces into her strong arms and kissed them in quite an undignified fashion. Aunt Tillie was a stickler for good manners, but when it came to expressing emotion, she didn't hold back. Perhaps she was loosening her reins in this fast-moving part of the world.

"Ladies," Teddy called as he stood by the carriage. "Ain't it a spectacular day?" He doffed his big felt hat in greeting once more and quickly replaced it on top of his red hair.

Libby grasped his callused hand as he helped her into the carriage. "Please, address us by our first names," she said. "We don't need to stand on ceremony." Once again she was recalling Robert Ealy's words: *Someone might shoot our legs from under us if we wait too long.*

She'd thought a lot about her short visit with the mayor's enigmatic nephew, his probing eyes and the odd bereavement she felt when his attention was drawn away. He would certainly not approve of her plans for the day.

She frowned, remembering his stormy face when he spoke of the "red devils" and of a brother named James killed in the conflict. She sighed. For some, war never seemed to end. It bloomed in a dark corner of the soul where it grew and festered. Surely that was no way to live.

Yet, what did she know of Robert's pain? What did she know of war? Had she ever seen a loved one cut down? Ever watched his blood seeping into the ground?

Meg's voice broke into her thoughts, and Libby wondered how long her sister had been speaking.

She turned her attention to Meg, whose hair was tucked neatly inside a bonnet trimmed with white clematis and yellow daisies. Wispy strands strayed around the soft curve of her cheek. With gloved hands clasped in the lap of her long brown skirt, she looked out across the waves of golden wheat. "Did you have a nice time at the tea?" Meg asked idly.

"It was good to see Aunt Tillie happily entertaining her friends," Libby replied. "And the pastries were quite good." She paused, considering her thoughts. "The parlor is beautifully appointed. I daresay we could not have seen a finer display in Boston or London."

When there was no immediate response, Libby realized that Meg really wanted to know about Mayor Quaid's nephew. "He wants to take us to see a concert with the famous Adelina Patti, who will sing selections from the opera *Rigoletto.* He's anxious to show us this city of Omaha of which his uncle is so proud."

Likely that was all Robert had in mind in spite of his flattery and intrusive, teasing manner. Europeans thought Americans were brash and too forward. Americans in Boston and Philadelphia thought the West was wild and ungovernable. *Who could say if they are right or not?*

"He couldn't take his eyes off you," Meg said quietly, hands still closed in her lap.

No tease or jealousy lived in the remark. Meg's words simply revealed her belief that her sister was beautiful and desirable while she herself was ordinary.

Libby nudged her elbow playfully. "Nonsense. He was being what people in this part of the world call 'neighborly.'" She gave Meg a sidelong look. "But he *was* handsome in that modern suit and jaunty cravat," she mused.

Wouldn't it be something if I end up making the match my mother so hopes for, way out here on the plains?

Meg raised an eyebrow and gave neither agreement nor rebuttal.

Libby realized that Meg didn't like him, which made her feel cross with her sister. Meg's judgment was usually reliable, but she had no good cause to dislike Robert Ealy.

"We're getting close to the arena," Libby said, glad to be diverted from Meg's disdain. The road was crowded with buggies, carriages, and buckboards as people wended their way toward the huge fenced field where conveyances of all descriptions were parked. Teddy untied his horse, then helped Libby and Meg down from the high-wheeled carriage.

He led them through the crowd toward the seating area. It seemed that the whole town had turned out. Men in wide hats and work boots trudged across the flattened grass. Women in homespun dresses pressed forward, bonnet strings flapping. Eager children tugged at grown-ups' hands.

"It's not far." Teddy pointed to a huge sign strung from two posts: Buffalo Bill's Wild West.

"The Colonel doesn't call it a 'show,' because that would make it sound cheap and ordinary," Teddy explained. "He says it's an original American amusement for family entertainment and the preservation of Old West traditions."

It seemed to Libby that Robert and Aunt Tillie's other friends shouldn't object to such ideals, but sometimes people could be shortsighted and more than a little snobbish.

"Is that part of a train?" Meg asked, pointing to a long, low car on which bright letters were painted: "Buffalo Bill's Wild West: Rough Riders, Horses and Horsemen, Military Action."

"Yup," Teddy said proudly. "They have a whole fleet of railroad cars for the troupe that travels with the Colonel. I hired on as a local roustabout, but I'm getting to know some of the performers."

People were filling the rough-hewn benches that circled a wide area surrounded by tents and teepees, wagons, animals, and people. There were buffalo, elk, mountain sheep, and hundreds of horses on the show lot. Performers in a variety of costumes lingered in the background, checking saddles, ropes, and weapons, or currying horses. There was an unusual mix of people, including American Indians, vaqueros, scouts, cowboys, and even some who looked like Russian gypsies.

Teddy found space in the second row of benches and instructed Libby and Meg to stay there until the end of the show. Then he left to collect his horse at the holding area and work his shift with the local stagehands behind the scenes.

Libby grabbed her sister's hand as the Cowboy Band played *The Star-Spangled Banner.* She gave a little gasp when a white canvas curtain opened and a band of Indians in full war paint dashed in on horseback. Their yells mingled with the jangling of bells around their ponies' necks. They pulled up a few feet from where Libby and Meg were seated, and the dust from their hooves swirled in the air. The curtain parted again, and cowboys dashed into view and flew down the track, waving their hats, then drawing up with a sudden halt.

With a flourish of trumpets, Buffalo Bill galloped down in front of the line on a magnificent white horse with a silver-studded bridle. His open coat flared in the breeze, revealing a bright crimson shirt and vest. He rode high in the saddle, French calfskin boots held fast in the iron stirrups. His long, wavy hair fell in platinum masses from a wide sombrero glistening gold in the sun.

"Ready? Go!" Cody shouted, and the line of men and animals turned instantly into a kaleidoscope of color. Indians rode full tilt around and around the arena, their feathers flying in the air. Cowboys and Mexicans, sometimes in the saddle and sometimes out of it, flew by in a blaze of color. If Teddy was among them, it was impossible to make out his features.

Libby sat spellbound, hearing Meg's excited gasps and her own exclamations as the barking of revolvers and the cracking of carbines ensued. It made her blood tingle. She had read about the dangerous and romantic Pony Express riders who carried mail across the Old West before the advent of trains, and of course about the great confrontation between the cowboys and the American Indians. Cody was a prominent figure in the daring accounts. His exploits were legendary.

Libby watched a series of skits in which the Old West was reenacted in startling detail. Then two of the most celebrated shooters in the United States, "Doc" Carver and Captain Bogardus, showed off their expertise by shooting glass balls out of the air.

A voice called attention to another staging area. "Ladies and gentlemen, Miss Lillian Smith, Champion Rifle Shot of the World."

A woman in tights and a revealing blouse came dancing out onto the stage, short dark hair peeking out from under her broad-brimmed hat. She pointed a gun at a tall man several paces away from her who had placed a potato on top of his sombrero. He wore leather trousers, high shiny boots, and a jacket of leopard skin.

Miss Smith stepped forward, took four paces toward the man, and shot the potato off his head. She curtsied grandly with a look of pride and whirled around to show off a costume that would have shocked Miss Goodwin to her haughty core.

Libby knew that exhibition shooters were not a new phenomenon. They dated at least to the early 1800s, when marksmen performed with circuses. They were growing more and more popular, and a number of them were women. *Aunt Tillie wouldn't like it,* Libby thought.

The next act was being announced. Libby hushed her disturbed thoughts as a man dubbed "the King of the Cowboys" threw a steer by the horns and tied it single-handedly. He was easily six-foot-four and rugged as a mountain slope.

She watched in amazement as a boy who looked to be no more than fifteen spun a rope high above his head. Then he twirled it down to the ground where he danced through it with remarkable ease.

"I think that's the Cowboy Kid," Meg whispered. "I heard that Cody adopted him, taught him to shoot, and made him a star. He's not much older than our little brother."

Libby pondered the boy's amazing skill, but she was straining her eyes for a glimpse of the man she'd helped along the road on the night of their arrival, the man Teddy thought was Sitting Bull. Indians with names like White Eagle, Walking Buffalo, Black Elk, and Red Shirt demonstrated their skills with the bow and arrow and rode their ponies around the arena, but none fit the image burned into her mind.

Suddenly, he appeared on a great horse—not a pony like the others rode, but a magnificent steed easily sixteen hands high. He didn't come whooping and galloping across the staging area as other performers had, but maintained a steady advance, bold and mesmerizing. A hush came over the audience at the sight of him in a headdress of large eagle feathers, a buckskin tunic heavily trimmed with beads, and a medicine bag at his side. He was still wearing his crucifix, an unexpected accoutrement among the bow and arrows and long peace pipe trimmed with ribbon.

People in the East wrote and talked about Sitting Bull, the Teton Sioux chief and holy man. He was famous, known for his bravery and dedication to his tribe. It was said that he had joined up with Buffalo Bill because he wanted "to see the new White Father at Washington," President Grover Cleveland, hoping he might intervene on behalf of his suffering people.

"Is it wrong for me to love my own?" he had been quoted

as saying. "Is it wicked for me because my skin is red? Because I am Sioux? Because I was born where my father lived? Because I would die for my people and my country?"

The audience watched respectfully. Libby stared at the solemn face, rigid and unsmiling. Indeed she was looking into the same piercing eyes that had opened on a strange white woman who was trying to bathe his wounded head. He did not turn to look at her, but rode steadily on and around the arena one more time to the applause of the crowd.

Meg tugged at her arm. "It's him, isn't it?" she whispered. "I'm so glad he's all right."

Libby nodded slowly. *What had happened to Sitting Bull that night?*

Teddy had said someone seemed intent on sabotaging the troupe, that "accidents" were taking place. But who would do that—and why?

Perhaps some disgruntled performer who had been let go was exacting his revenge. Libby felt a stab of worry for Teddy, who had quickly become a friend. However, perhaps the accidents were really just accidents.

"They treat me like family," Teddy had said on their way to the show. "The Colonel is one of the kindest men I know. And he's doing what he can for the Indians. He gets them off the reservation and pays them well. He really respects them, despite his service as a military scout." Teddy had set his chin firmly. "And he never shot an Indian unless his life was threatened."

That was reason enough for Libby to like the scout-turned-showman and to wish his Wild West show well. When he came riding into the arena once more, waving his hat and saluting the audience, it seemed to Libby that he looked at her with surprising directness. His glorious hair gleamed in the sun as he passed by, and the crowd roared with enthusiasm.

As the performers took another turn around the arena, Cody flung his hat toward each as though to introduce them and invite applause. Libby clapped heartily, restraining herself from shouting her approval.

Teddy would collect them when the last of the performers left the arena, and they would go back to Aunt Tillie's homestead. But Libby knew she would be eager to witness the exciting drama all over again.

She had turned to share her enthusiasm with Meg when the Cowboy Kid came riding in for his "curtain call," pointing his pistols skyward and sending up a volley of shots. The audience roared approval as his bullets shattered clay pigeons while he stood on his head and executed other amazing tricks. When his act neared an end, he bowed from the waist grandly and threw his hat high in the air, catching it neatly when it fell. Libby clapped with delight.

Suddenly, the Cowboy Kid's horse reared, tossed its head erratically, and reared again, throwing him to the ground. A gasp went up from the audience.

Libby sat transfixed as the horse shook its mane and trotted off, leaving the boy on the ground, still and unmoving. The Cowboy Kid—Johnny Baker, Buffalo Bill's ward—was carried away on swift feet through the white canvas curtain.

Another accident?

9

Cabot Falls, Vermont
Present Day

Sofia had never met Rathbone Steele in person, but the moment he stepped into the library later that day, she knew she was looking at Howahkan's irascible agent. The barrel-chested man stopped momentarily in the entryway and removed a derby hat from a head of slightly too-long gray hair that curled at his collar. He squared his shoulders and proceeded to the desk, where she stood with Marla.

He had to be in his late fifties, Sofia guessed, taking in his sculpted sideburns and silver-framed glasses. His three-piece charcoal suit, neatly pressed, gave no indication that he'd been sitting on a plane from New York City or driving from Boston to Cabot Falls on a warm afternoon. He stopped at the desk and set his briefcase on the floor.

"I'm here to see Mrs. Sofia Parker," he said, his voice low and scratchy, as if he might have a cold.

Steele, who was close to the same height as Sofia and slightly shorter than Marla, scrutinized them with penetrating eyes as iron-gray as his hair. He unbuttoned his coat with carefully groomed fingers. Shiny cuff links flashed from his immaculate white shirt, adding to the impression of fastidiousness. "I'm Rathbone Steele. I believe I am expected," he said, addressing Sofia.

"Yes, I'm Sofia Parker." She extended her hand and felt the

cool, brief pressure of his palm. The heavy sweetness of his cologne wafted toward her in heady waves. Sofia stepped back instinctively. "And this is Marla Dixon, head librarian and a member of the art show committee."

"I would have been here sooner, but I had to check in immediately with your police department the moment I got here. Nasty business," he said.

Nasty business? Where was his outrage over a fallen artist—a young artist whom he obviously knew well enough to represent and foster?

"We're pleased to meet you," Sofia said, trying not to be put off by his cavalier manner. Everyone handled grief differently. "I'm very sorry for your loss, Mr. Steele," she said, giving him a penetrating look that seemed to bring him up short.

He drew what might have been a steadying breath. "Howahkan was a brilliant artist and a friend. He had a great career in front of him." He made a little half turn and stared off into some neutral space. "He was a troubled man. I tried to help him." He sighed. "It's hard to believe that he decided to end his life."

Sofia let a few seconds of silence pass. Indeed, it did appear that Howahkan had ended his own life, but why all the mystery if that was so? What was Officer Quimby not saying?

Before the young officer had hauled Homer Winslow in for questioning, Sofia had confronted Homer about the comment he made about Howahkan's barrette.

Homer had all but sobbed when faced with his unfortunate comment. "All right! All right!" he had finally confessed. "I was there. But I only wanted to get a look at him. I hung around in the lobby until I saw him come in. But I didn't try to talk to him, and I didn't go to his room."

"What happened next?" Officer Quimby had asked in a level tone.

"He went to the desk and got his key. Then he went into the gift shop and bought a can of something and took the exit to the stairs. I don't know what his room number was, and I didn't follow him. I swear it."

Sofia knew Homer had been against bringing the guest artist to the show and that he was a bigoted little man, but would he try to harm him?

We don't think he was alone in that hotel room, Officer Quimby had said, but he didn't discuss his reasons for thinking so. In spite of the note left behind, did he suspect that Howahkan hadn't committed suicide? But who would want to do away with the young artist? And how had the artist died? The questions plagued her.

"I shouldn't have let him travel alone. That much is clear," Steele said, bringing Sofia back to the present moment. She studied his smooth forehead and the bushy brows that hovered low over almond-shaped eyes.

"I should have gotten on the flight with him, but I had some business that couldn't be put off," Steele continued. "If only I had." He left off saying that he might have been able to prevent Howahkan's death. He cleared his throat as if to bring an end to the unfortunate affair and then raised an eyebrow. "Ladies, is there somewhere we can go to discuss our business?"

"Of course." Marla drew a key from the pocket of her jacket. "Follow us, please," she said with a wary glance at Sofia.

Marla signaled for one of the librarians to take her place at the desk, where visitors were converging in significant numbers. Everyone wanted to know what had happened. Marla led the agent into the reading room where Howahkan's paintings were displayed on carefully prepared mounts around the perimeter. Steele paused at the first painting and crossed his arms over his broad chest. The painting portrayed a young cowboy with a sketch pad on his knees. In the background, horses grazed serenely. Near the man's booted feet lay a saddle, which might recently have been removed from one of the animals' muscular backs. "That one, ladies, depicts Howahkan's great-grandfather," Steele said.

Why did he insist on calling them "ladies" as though they were a hundred years old? Sofia wasn't sure why Steele irritated her so much, but his ponderous pronouncements invaded the room where Howahkan seemed a virtual presence.

"This was when his great-grandfather was a young man, of course," Steele said. "When Theodore Blane wasn't taming bucking broncos or herding steers, he liked to sketch all kinds of Old West scenes." He pointed with a carefully groomed forefinger. "This painting was made from a self-portrait of Mr. Blane."

Sofia studied the face of the young cowboy with his thatch of red hair and patrician nose. Obviously Caucasian. The brochure indicated that he had eventually married a Sioux princess, which was unusual for those times when hostilities were still running high. Howahkan's great-grandfather and great-grandmother must have been exceptional people, willing to fly in the face of convention. She wished she could have known them.

Steele frowned as he looked at the next painting of a young maiden with silken black hair, crouched along the edge of a stream. Little of the face could be seen, but one could not help but be touched by her grace and beauty. Sofia hadn't been able to get the image out of her mind after she'd unwrapped the painting. Who was she? Had Howahkan loved her? Lost her, perhaps? Could that explain his deep melancholy?

"What are you doing?" Marla's raised voice broke into her thoughts.

Sofia turned to see Rathbone Steele systematically removing each of the price cards from beneath the paintings—cards they had painstakingly affixed in preparation for the show.

"Well, ladies, you don't think we would let these go at such meager prices. Now that Howahkan is dead, they are worth infinitely more."

"But we agreed," Sofia said. "We chose to showcase Howahkan's art not only because it's remarkably good but because it's affordable for our patrons. This isn't New York City, you know."

"It wouldn't be fair to raise the prices now," Marla agreed vigorously.

Sofia felt her pulse race. "In any case, we can't even talk about opening a show here until funeral arrangements are made. We need to know who's in line to inherit and what that person's wishes are. Maybe he or she doesn't want to sell these paintings."

"That is not the point," Steele said. The deft movements of his hands emphasized the gold cuff links with their small, whitish stones.

The man has expensive tastes, Sofia thought. *A champagne appetite on a beer income?* How much, she wondered, did he stand to gain from the sale of Howahkan's work?

"Details can be worked out at a later date concerning any heirs," Steele said, "but your contract is with Steele and Steele Agency." He proffered a generous smile. "And, ladies, I expect that contract to be honored as promised."

Sofia stared at him, stunned. How could he carry on with Howahkan dead and his family—if he had any—still unaware?

"The poor boy was really quite alone in the world," Steele said, bowing his well-coiffed head briefly. "His education was sponsored by the government because of his Native American ancestry, but we recognized his talent and took him under our wing—at considerable expense, I might add."

"What about his family?" she asked. "Surely there must be someone."

Steele tucked the price cards inside his jacket, pausing once more by the painting of the young woman. "There is a sister in upstate New York, but she has nothing to do with him. I can assure you she will rejoice to have him out of her life permanently. She goes by the charming name of Willow June. No doubt the Sioux influence. Married name, I believe, is Hunt." He pressed his lips together in distaste.

Sofia was too stunned to say anything, but Steele wasn't finished.

"They are quite clearly estranged. She blames Howahkan for their parents' death. He was driving at the time, and both were killed in a fiery crash." Steele sighed. "Poor Skylar never got over it." He crossed his arms over his chest. The dark eyes sparked angrily. "And his sister never forgave him. So much for the sweet Willow June."

It took a moment for Sofia to orient herself to Howahkan's real name—Skylar, Skylar Blane. *How terrible,* she thought. *To be all alone in the world and filled with self-recrimination.* "Well, they will have to locate her as next of kin," Sofia said, more to herself than to anyone. "Regardless of their relationship, she'll have to be notified."

"I told the police what I know. No doubt they'll find her, but there's no reason why the show should be put off. It may seem very harsh to you, but life does go on, and time is money." Steele raised his bushy brows and peered over his spectacles as he moved to the conference table. "Skylar's death will only heighten interest."

"Howahkan," Sofia whispered, as though using the name he preferred made up for the grave injustice. It was heartbreaking, how callous the art world could be, that death was an opportunity to exploit an artist for gain. Sofia sighed. "We had the approval of the library board," she said quietly, "but there may be trouble now. Something has happened that may change—"

An insistent knock sent Marla to the door of the reading room. "I distinctly asked that we not be disturbed," she grumbled under her breath.

The volunteer librarian mumbled an apology and stood wringing her hands and rolling her eyes. Her lips framed the words *Winifred Winslow*.

And then the formidable woman stormed past the librarian and into the reading room. She headed directly for Sofia, who remained seated at the table with Rathbone Steele. "Well," she began, dark eyes flashing in a heavily made-up face very like her son's. "I hope you're happy. My Homer is devastated."

Sofia stared at the woman teetering on the three-inch heels she insisted on wearing though she was past sixty. She was wearing clothes sold in her boutique and designed for women half her age. The pink ruffled blouse and tight linen skirt did little to enhance her stout figure.

"It's your fault the police arrested him," she said, pointing a finger at Sofia. Her face bloomed as pink as her blouse. "He was too sick even to open the shop today."

"Mrs. Winslow," Sofia began, "I had to tell the police what I knew. Besides, Homer wasn't arrested. He was only questioned, as were the rest of us."

"He was interrogated like a common criminal," Winifred accused.

Sofia drew in a breath. "He was seen at the hotel where the artist died," she said quietly. "He may not have had anything to do with what happened, but he shouldn't have lied about being there." Sofia exchanged glances with Marla, who had grown slightly pale.

"I never should have agreed to this ridiculous show. The whole town will be gossiping," Winifred wailed. Then she seemed to deflate like a spent balloon. "If it wasn't for Homer,

I'd insist that we shut the whole thing down right now." She looked as though she might cry, seriously endangering her heavy black mascara.

Rathbone Steele rose and went to Winifred with both hands extended. "Allow me to introduce myself. I represent the Steele and Steele Agency of New York City, and I'm honored to meet the chairman of the Cabot Falls Library Board." His voice dripped with sweetness as he bowed his silvery head. "I'm Rathbone Steele," he went on, for Winifred had been struck silent. "And let me say, I've seen Mr. Winslow's paintings, and he has a certain flair, a scintillating way with color that we don't often see in the art world."

Sofia was struck by how quickly he had assessed Winifred's character and planned his approach.

"I should know, dear lady," Steele continued, "because I also represent Howahkan, esteemed painter of western art, God rest his soul. And let me say how much we at the agency appreciate showcasing his art here in Cabot Falls along with the work of fine local artists like your son."

Liar, liar, pants on fire, Sofia thought.

If a person could be said to visibly melt, that would have described Winifred Winslow. She made a bold attempt at speech but managed only to mumble through trembling pink lips. She finally cleared her throat. "Since everyone is expecting it and all the plans have been made, we might as well." She shifted her considerable weight from one foot to the other and looked sheepishly at Marla and Sofia.

"Mr. Steele has agreed to stay and represent Howahkan's work in the absence of the artist," Marla said, her jaw clenched.

Sofia could see the fire in her blue eyes. *Agreed?* He had demanded that they carry through with the terms of their contract.

"Then I suppose the show should go on." Winifred crooned, blushing in the wake of Rathbone Steele's flattery. "Instead of

Thursday through Saturday, we could begin tonight and go through Saturday."

"Splendid!" Steele said. "Splendid, dear lady." And he actually kissed her pudgy hand.

"This whole business is so . . . distressing," Winifred said haltingly. But she was clearly flattered, and Sofia knew there would be no trouble from her, at least so long as Rathbone Steele was in the picture.

After Marla had ushered the lady from the room, Steele also took his leave abruptly. He gave them his card and said he could be reached at the Cabot Falls Inn.

"He's quite the schmoozer, isn't he?" Marla said, turning to Sofia with arms folded across her chest.

The way he'd worked Winifred Winslow was nothing short of masterful. If anyone could "help" Howahkan along the path to the Great Spirit, it was probably not beyond the skill and cunning of Rathbone Steele. Sofia let her breath out in a long stream. But luckily for him, he'd been miles away from Cabot Falls at the time. *And too bad for me, because I'd like to strangle him.*

"I'm sure he had to prove he wasn't anywhere near Cabot Falls when Howahkan died," Marla said thoughtfully. "But I bet he's been told not to leave town. Until the cause of death has been clearly confirmed, the police will be looking very closely at everyone involved with our departed guest artist."

Sofia nodded, thinking about the estranged sister and wondering if Officer Quimby had located her yet. Was she indeed the bitter, unforgiving woman Steele made her out to be? *If so, Rathbone was right—she will rejoice to have him out of her life permanently.* She glanced at the clock on the wall and raised an eyebrow at Marla. "I'm going to have a talk with Officer Quimby. Care to tag along?"

"I'm in," Marla said. "I'm for anything to get this thing settled and get back to normal, whatever that is."

10

Omaha, Nebraska
June 1885

"They're absolutely beautiful." Libby stroked the tiny puppy in her arms with a gentle finger. Five more pups nuzzled Duchess among the soft bedclothes in a large wicker basket on Aunt Tillie's porch. Their little mouths worked eagerly as they struggled to nurse, butting their oversized heads against their mother.

"They certainly are precious," Libby said. "Although they don't have much hair, do they?"

"Before long they'll have curls as beautiful as their mother's," Tillie said. "It's her second litter, so she's quite an expert now." She leaned down and clucked her tongue affectionately in the dog's curly black ear. "Aren't you, girl?"

Libby waited with Aunt Tillie on the broad stone porch, which Tillie liked to call "the veranda," expecting the imminent arrival of Robert Ealy's carriage. He was to escort them to the concert featuring the well-known opera singer.

"Imagine Meg becoming ill," Tillie said, pursing her lips in a pout. "She won't get to hear the talented Miss Patti at our new civic auditorium. That building was completed only last year," she raved, clasping her gloved hands in the lap of her pink silk dress with its tightly fitting bodice. "It cost more than $100,000."

Early that afternoon, Meg had complained of a mild stomachache and had gone to lie down. She'd refused lunch and declared a little later that she didn't feel well enough to go to the concert. "You go along with Aunt Tillie," she had said. "Don't worry about me. Greta will look after me. It's really nothing serious, but I don't think I should go out."

Now Libby frowned, thinking about the exchange with Meg. She knew Meg loved music, but her sister hadn't expressed much enthusiasm for the company of Robert Ealy. Was she really not well? Or had she deliberately chosen to stay home to avoid him? Perhaps she was standing aside to give Robert a freer rein to court her sister's affections. Libby sighed and drew a long breath. "Aunt Tillie, what do you know about Mr. Ealy?"

Aunt Tillie adjusted the ribbon on her hat. "I know he is quite taken with you," she said with a little smile. "As well he should be, charming girl that you are. And the nephew of our esteemed mayor is certainly a handsome gentleman." She paused and wrinkled her forehead in thought. "Mr. Ealy is somewhat new to our state. He came up from Texas way, I believe."

Texas, she thought. *Teddy is from Texas, but the two certainly don't dress or talk in the same fashion.*

Tillie fell silent, and Libby wondered if her aunt knew anything about Robert at all, beyond his social standing. That she was impressed with him was clear. Status was important to Tillie—to a lot of people, she supposed. Back East or out West.

"In time he'll make a fine contribution to our expanding community," Tillie said. "I told your mother I would show you the best of the West." She chuckled and waved an embroidered fan across her face. "Wasn't it kind of Robert to make arrangements for the concert? Imagine, Adelina Patti, right here in Omaha."

"Indeed," Libby responded. "Mr. Ealy has been most attentive.

Meg and I are fortunate to experience many interesting aspects of the West, including Buffalo Bill's demonstration that you kindly arranged for us to visit with Teddy."

"I did no such arranging," she countered. "I only *allowed* you to go, unwisely, and I was repaid with your lateness in returning. I'm told I am far too lenient with my staff. I ought to adhere more closely to social boundaries, such as those between you and that young cowboy."

Like Libby's mother, Aunt Tillie was far too concerned with class and the perception of her peers. But Libby's mind was too full of the exciting sights and sounds she had witnessed to concern herself with social etiquette.

The arena had been nearly empty when Teddy returned to collect them. He was unusually subdued. "Is the Cowboy Kid all right?" she had asked, eager to know what had happened after the young man was thrown from his horse and carried off into one of the Wild West tents.

"He's okay, I think," Teddy had responded, blue eyes clouding. "Got a mighty bump on his head, but he came to once we got him backstage." He shook his head. "Johnny ain't never been throwed before," he mused.

"Was it an accident?" Libby had pressed, remembering Sitting Bull's mishap and what Teddy had said about the trouble at the arena.

"Nope," Teddy had said with a long sigh. "Somebody stuck a burr under his horse's saddle blanket. The Colonel's hopping mad. It ain't just that Johnny's one of the most popular acts. He's real special to the Colonel."

Now Libby shook her head in a vain effort to dispel the echo of Teddy's words. She turned to Aunt Tillie, who was fanning herself on the veranda and watching for Robert's carriage. "Teddy was only late because one of the cowboys from the show got hurt. I just hope nothing else happens." She pursed her lips thoughtfully. "Why do you think someone would cause trouble for Colonel Cody, Aunt Tillie?"

"Who knows why people do what they do?" Tillie said wearily. "Some people don't like Mr. Cody hiring on all those Indians. It makes them nervous."

"Teddy says Colonel Cody respects them and wants to help them. He encourages the wives and children of his Indian performers to set up camp as they would in their homeland. It's part of the show," Libby said. "He wants the paying public to see the human side of the 'fierce warriors,' that they have families like anyone else, and their own distinct traditions."

But there was no more time to consider the matter of Buffalo Bill Cody's troubles. Aunt Tillie rose, gently tucking a blanket over Duchess's basket. "There's our Robert now. Put all that cowboy nonsense out of your head and enjoy some real culture."

Robert Ealy emerged from the carriage in a dark tailcoat and ascot that Libby saw with surprise closely matched the blue of her dress. As he bowed and removed his top hat, she felt her cheeks grow warm. Had he marked the odd coincidence? His light hair shone, giving him a dazzling appearance as he graciously greeted them and helped them board the high-wheeled carriage.

They rode over mostly unpaved roads, Robert pointing out various landmarks, including a rambling building in a pasture on the outskirts of the city. "That's Creighton University, founded in '78," he said.

"A fine institution," Aunt Tillie interjected. "It was fortuitous that President Lincoln chose to take the transcontinental railroad through here and not down in Missouri. Otherwise we probably would never have developed into such a fine metropolitan area."

"Indeed," Robert said. "And there is the auditorium." He pointed to an impressive Italianate brick building on a flat, grassy area where a few trees, still in their infancy, had been planted. The carriage rolled into a hitching area joining horses and as many as fifty buggies, buckboards, and coaches.

"I'm sorry your sister is unwell," he said in that husky tone that had first unsettled Libby, "but I'm pleased that you and your dear aunt could join us for this event, one of the first to be held in the new auditorium." He paused, turning to her. "May I compliment you on your lovely gown? We look as though we belong together." Before she could react to his presumptuous remark, he added, "Now we must hurry in before all of the best seats are taken."

Plain wooden chairs faced the platform in a modified arc. A Broadwood grand piano of rich mahogany dominated the stage framed by burgundy velvet drapes.

Aunt Tillie led the way, pulling Libby after her by the hand so that she was left to sit next to Robert. The crowd gathered and conversed in hushed tones as they awaited the singer and her accompanist.

"Miss Patti is highly acclaimed in the music capitals of Europe," Aunt Tillie whispered. "A truly magnificent soprano. I do believe she's as accomplished as Miss Jenny Lind and Thérèsa Tietjens." She craned her head slightly. "Ah, there is our mayor."

Libby followed her gaze to the portly man in black tailcoat and tie, his face as florid as it had been in her aunt's parlor, the mutton chops as full and silvery.

His small, flat feet bore his bulk steadily forward to the center of the stage. He raised his hands in a gesture intended to still the crowd and then clasped his hands over his stomach and cleared his throat.

"Allow me to greet you on behalf of the great city of Omaha, and with all deference to the engineers of this fine establishment, where tonight we will hear the magnificent tones of the magnificent Miss Adelina Patti. She will be singing arias from the immensely popular *Rigoletto*, Verdi's significant opera. Please greet Miss Patti and her accompanist, Mr. Edward Delevan."

As the young man took his place at the pianoforte, the audience applauded vigorously; a few cheered without restraint. Even Aunt Tillie gave refined little gasps of pleasure as the shapely soprano, dressed in a rich caramel-colored gown and jeweled headpiece, emerged. As the music began, she clasped her hands demurely and lifted her elegant head.

When the first aria ended, the audience erupted in applause. Libby turned to find Robert's expectant gaze on her. "Did I not say you would be delighted?" he remarked, placing a hand lightly on her arm. She snugged her shawl around her shoulders, dislodging his hand politely.

Miss Patti sang three more pieces and an encore. When she finally exited to the wings, the mayor went quickly to center stage, clapping as he walked, his round face reddening even more. "I'm sure we are all honored to have Miss Patti here today. She will appear in Lincoln tomorrow for a gala performance."

When the applause began again, the mayor silenced them with a wave of his hand. "But before you go"—he gave a small bow—"we are very proud of our fair city, friends," the mayor said. "Indeed, we have come a long way from building soddies on the prairie as our parents and even some of you did in days gone by."

More nods and cheers of affirmation arose from the crowd. The mayor seemed to be building toward something and kept poking his head out of his collar like a nervous turtle. From the corner of her eye, Libby saw Robert lean forward and hold the edge of his chair rigidly as if anticipating something of which he might disapprove.

Libby recalled the strain she had witnessed between the two men in Aunt Tillie's parlor. Perhaps the argument involved young ideas versus traditional conventions. Or was there something else? She felt Robert's reserve as he sat stiffly in his seat.

"I take nothing away from our pioneer forebears, ladies and gentlemen, especially those who tamed the West and opened it for new growth and civilization." The mayor stretched out of his collar once more. He was perspiring, and his face shone as though some misplaced glory rested on him.

"Now, some of you have heard of an excellent demonstration taking place at the arena south of our fair city to commemorate those colorful days of the Old West. And here to tell you a little about it . . ." He made a slight turn on his dainty feet and gestured toward stage left.

Robert rose halfway in his seat, head erect, eyes fixed on his uncle. He looked anything but pleased.

Suddenly, a shot rang out and a great gasp went up from the audience. A lone figure erupted from the wings, a tall man with shoulder-length hair that cascaded like a waterfall from under a white sombrero. Resplendent in a fiery red shirt, Buffalo Bill faced the audience, gun aimed at the ceiling.

"Ladies and gentlemen," he said when the clapping waned, "forgive this intrusion on your musical enjoyment, but I'm here to extend an invitation to my western extravaganza tomorrow."

His broad smile and stunning looks seemed to cast a spell over the crowd. When he paused and looked searchingly into the audience, Libby felt his penetrating gaze fall on her. She drew a startled breath. It was much the same look he'd given her when he passed by her in the arena. Did he know she was the one who had stopped to help Sitting Bull?

"I promise you frontier entertainment like no other," the colonel continued. "We'll reenact for you scenes of the Old West, Indian raids, fancy shooting, and bronc busting. You'll meet a little girl named Annie Oakley who can shoot the feathers off an arrow at fifty yards. 'Little Missie' comes all the way from Darke County, Ohio. She can shoot farther and straighter than any gunfighter in the world. Believe me, you won't be disappointed."

When he disappeared into the wings, a renewed burst of applause came from the audience. It died down, and people began to filter out of the theater. The concert was over.

"I told him not to." Robert was furious. He rose to his feet and stared at the averted face of his uncle, who was shaking hands and exchanging greetings with departing guests.

Told him not to what? Not to allow "that ruffian" to appear and give an announcement? Libby was perplexed.

Robert turned his back to the stage and moved to the door without waiting for Libby or Aunt Tillie to follow. Was it Buffalo Bill and the Wild West demonstration that he and his uncle had been arguing about that day in Tillie's parlor? Had the Colonel's potential "advertisement" been discussed? Why was Robert so incensed?

Outside the auditorium, Robert appeared to recover himself. He helped the women with their wraps and gestured for them to move ahead of him to the carriage. They had almost reached it when a rider on horseback came galloping toward them and stopped short at Libby's side.

Astonished, she looked up to see Buffalo Bill gazing down at her from his magnificent horse. He was holding something out toward her. "These are free passes for you and the other young lady. Your sister, I believe. With my compliments and those of Little Missie."

Having placed the small pieces of paper in Libby's gloved hands, he galloped off, his long plume of hair flying beneath the white sombrero.

11

Omaha, Nebraska
June 1885

*L*ibby studied her image in the mirror. The riding habit she had received for her sixteenth birthday was only a little tight in the bodice. The skirt and high-buttoned jacket were a dark, lush green and made of a sturdy fabric. Elastic straps kept the matching breeches in place under her high-top boots. She would wear a lightweight chemisette and leave the tapered jacket unbuttoned to allow freer movement.

She had agreed to go riding on Aunt Tillie's property with Robert Ealy. It was a splendid day, but it was the thought of Queen, silky black mane flying in the breeze, that brought a thrill of excitement.

"Are you sure you won't go along with us, Meg?" Libby asked. "You do look so much better."

"I'm feeling quite well," Meg said, drawing a morning gown of pale pink over her head, "but I promised Sonja I would show her the scarf I've been making. She loves needlework, and it will be so much fun to embroider together."

"You've been spending a lot of time with Sonja and her mother," Libby mused. Meg chose her companions without concern for their social status, a quality unpopular with both their mother and their aunt.

"Sonja is going to teach me how to bake that delicious

cardamom sweet bread she and her mother make," Meg said, sitting down to button her slippers. She smiled up at Libby's reflection in Aunt Tillie's walnut-framed oval mirror. "You don't mind really, do you?" she asked softly. "I'm not much for riding horses."

"I always prefer your company to your absence," Libby said, meaning it. She looked at her sister fondly. "I'm sorry you missed the concert, Meg. Miss Patti was superb, and the new auditorium was lovely." Libby paused as she tied a small leather reticule to her waistband. "It was everything Aunt Tillie said it would be."

"I'm sure it was wonderful," Meg said, gentle eyes brightening. "But I wish I had seen that dashing Colonel Cody come striding onto the platform with his gun blazing as you described. He must have brought down the house."

"I think his show has become quite popular," Libby said. "As Teddy pointed out, many people in town, including the mayor, look at Cody's Rough Riders with favor. Certainly, if it brings people into town, it can only enhance the expanding community's profits." She paused, puzzling once more over Robert's reaction, his quick anger and the way he had stormed out of the auditorium.

On the trip home he had been distant. His behavior might even have been considered rude. Without Aunt Tillie's continuous chatter, it would have been awkward indeed. Yet, when they had sipped a post-concert lemonade on Tillie's porch, he seemed to forget any unpleasantness, and he regaled them with descriptions of life in the rapidly developing West.

When Aunt Tillie excused herself to retire, Robert had detained Libby on the porch, his unusual eyes gleaming turquoise in the advancing twilight. "I'm very glad you enjoyed the concert," he said. "Your company made this evening very special." He had taken her hand and gently brought it to his lips. His gentlemanly manner and tender touch had stirred something both delightful and vaguely troubling.

"Did he really do that?"

Libby looked up to see Meg's quizzical expression. "I'm sorry," she said, realizing she hadn't heard her sister's question. "Do what?"

"Colonel Cody. Did he really come galloping up to Mr. Ealy's carriage to find you after the concert?"

"Like a knight dashing into the fray," Libby affirmed, laughing. "I daresay I've never seen anything like it. I'm afraid Robert was quite put out by his daring behavior."

"And no doubt by his attentions to you," Meg said with a smile that didn't quite reach her expressive hazel eyes.

"Hardly that," Libby said uncomfortably. "But look!" She went to the dressing table where she had put the free passes Cody had given her and handed one to Meg.

"They're free passes to the Wild West show. He looked right into my eyes and said they were for me and for 'the other young lady. Your sister, I believe.' Meg, he knows who we are."

"Do you suppose Teddy told him about Sitting Bull?" Meg asked.

"Yes, that must be how he knows that we tried to help him." Libby studied the ticket in her hand, wondering about its odd spattering of holes, as though someone had shot it through with bullets.

Libby frowned and gave a little shrug. "At least someone was grateful. Sitting Bull wasn't. He acted as though we were his enemies, but we were only trying to help. He seemed so angry when he got up and walked away." She cocked her head as another thought occurred to her. "First that old Indian gets hurt, and then the Cowboy Kid is thrown from his horse. He could have been trampled. No doubt he would have been if Teddy and the others hadn't acted quickly to get him out of harm's way." Libby looked down at the ticket in her hand again, recalling what Buffalo Bill had said. *Annie Oakley, a little girl who can shoot the feathers off an arrow at fifty yards.*

"Do you suppose she's like the girl in the tights who shot a potato off that man's head?" Libby mused aloud.

Teddy had told her that Miss Smith wasn't popular among the other performers. Although she was a good shot, she was spoiled and troublesome. "Annie Oakley? She's different," he had said. "She was raised in a Quaker family in Ohio and taught herself to shoot after her father died. Family would have starved otherwise."

"I rather think she's different from Miss Smith," Libby said. "Teddy says she's very kind and ladylike and that she sends her salary home to Ohio."

Meg raised a delicate eyebrow. "I didn't much like that immodest lady sharpshooter," she said. "If Miss Goodwin saw her, she'd need smelling salts to recover."

Libby picked up her hat from the dressing table. She looked beyond Meg to peer through the window above the bed. "I wonder what it would be like to do something extraordinary like Annie Oakley did for her family. Something all on your own that no one else dares to do." She sighed deeply at herself in the mirror, put on her hat, and bid her sister farewell.

"Have a good ride," Meg said. "And Libby, do be careful."

"Meg, dear, we'll be right here on Aunt Tillie's land. Besides, I have no intention of losing my head over him or anyone else."

"Sonja says . . ." Meg stopped. She looked down at her hands and gave a little shrug.

Meg didn't need to be ashamed of her friendship with the maid. "You and Sonja enjoy your visit," Libby said, kissing her quickly on the cheek.

The sky was a clear cornflower blue and the distant prairie

a waving field of gold as Libby made her way toward the barn. Queen circled the corral, lifting her elegant head to sniff the air. Several other horses grazed nearby. A sense of anticipation filled Libby. It was good to be alive on such a day.

As she neared the stable, she heard the sound of low voices. She hesitated, stepped back, and peered through the half-open door to see two men engaged in conversation. Robert Ealy, clad in a gentleman's riding habit, stood a few paces from a man with a dark mustache and brooding face. It was the cowboy called Hawk, who had so rudely taunted Teddy.

Perplexed, she watched until Robert's eye suddenly caught hers. He took a small step back as if surprised, stepped forward again, and wagged a finger in Hawk's face. "It's strictly forbidden to smoke in the stable," he said loudly. "And I must also ask what you're doing idle at this time in the morning. Why aren't you out on the range where you belong?"

Hawk's sullen eyes narrowed. The lines in his forehead deepened under Robert's censure. He glared at his accuser, then at Libby, and swept unruly hair off his forehead. He dropped his cigarette and crushed it with his boot before he spoke. "I got back late from a cattle drive," he muttered through gritted teeth. "I was on my way out."

"Of course you were," Robert said caustically. "Mrs. Primm will have to be advised of this breach."

Hawk's face a mix of puzzlement and defiance as Robert drew Libby away.

Libby was unsettled by the interchange. Yet she felt a sense of triumph at Hawk's debasement, retribution for the way he had treated Teddy, calling him "Teddy Bear" and "stable boy," and referring to her and Meg as "fancy ladies." Robert had taken it on himself to look out for Aunt Tillie's interests. That was something to be commended.

"These uncouth cowhands," Robert scoffed, taking Libby's elbow and steering her around muddy puddles near the corral gate. "He could have burnt the place down."

When Teddy emerged from the far side of the stable, Robert called out to him. "I hope we can trust you to saddle two adequate mounts for Miss Carson and me," he said gruffly.

Libby couldn't help but rush to Teddy's defense. "My aunt is very fond of Teddy. She says he is completely trustworthy." She smiled in Teddy's direction. "And he is the soul of kindness."

Robert gave a slight bow of accession and pulled his features into a smile. "As you say, dear lady." He gestured for her to step inside the corral, where Teddy was saddling Queen for her. Deferring Robert's hand, she mounted with Teddy's help, draping her legs off to the left beneath her long green skirt. "Thank you, Teddy."

Libby found it interesting that in the 1600s, it had been perfectly acceptable for women to ride astride. But through the 1700s, a lady straddling a horse grew less acceptable, and by the Regency era, any woman doing so was considered of questionable moral character. Libby was content to ride sidesaddle. Though with Miss Amelia Bloomer's new fashions, it would be quite easy and considerably more fun to ride as the men did.

Robert, handsome in a Norfolk jacket and tweed breeches, rode a tall steed with mane and tail of the same gleaming black as its muscled body. He set a slow pace, and they traveled across meadows blooming with wildflowers and the invasive sumac plant. On each side of the trail, bluestem grasses grew, some nearly six feet tall. In the distance, a few bison roamed.

It was easy to imagine the Mahas along with the Pawnee, Otoe, and Sioux tribes hunting there, riding their ponies freely over the territory, holding council with Meriwether Lewis and William Clark in 1804, trading their furs at the post established eight years later. "That's how Omaha got its name, isn't it?" she asked Robert. "From the Maha Indians?"

"*Omaha* means 'the upriver people' or 'against the current.' I suppose that's because the Indians moved against the current, upriver on the Mississippi. And they've been going against our current ever since," he added with decided distaste.

"Robert, this country is so vast, so sweeping," she remarked, hoping to lighten his mood.

"I know," he said. "The early settlers struggled bravely to win the land against terrible resistance."

Is he still thinking of the Indians who killed his brother? Libby frowned. She didn't want to speak war on such a glorious day. Or any day. The conversation lapsed, and they rode in silence but for the slow thud of horse hooves on the soft ground. A single cottonwood tree appeared a few yards ahead.

"Perhaps we might sit and enjoy the view for a little while," Robert suggested. "Mrs. Primm insisted I take a canteen along with cold well water and some of her homemade lemon cakes."

"That would be very nice," Libby said. Though they'd only been riding forty minutes or so, she was feeling a slight cramp in her left leg and welcomed a rest.

Robert helped her down, unrolled a woolen blanket, and spread it on a level swatch of short grass. He looped their horses' reins to the cottonwood and extracted the water and cakes from his saddlebag.

She took the cup he offered and a small slice of lemon cake, which he served on a linen handkerchief. "Oh, this is wonderful," she said, retrieving a stray crumb from her lap. "What is it about the open air that makes food taste so good?"

He smiled. "Wide open spaces and friends to inhabit them," he said, taking a bite of lemon cake. He chewed thoughtfully and let a little silence fall between them. Then he looked at her intently, smiling, though a frown wrinkled his forehead. "Miss Elizabeth, Libby, what will you do when your holiday is over?"

The question caught her off guard. *What indeed?* Her course of studies had ended, and she had thought of teaching or tutoring. Society offered little else to a young woman. Of course, there was marriage, the one course always open to a woman who could impress a man. But she so wanted to do something on her own. Something to make a difference in the world. *It isn't that marriage and family are not fine aspirations.*

He was sitting so close, the sun sparking off the unusual pin in his tie. She looked away, unnerved by Robert's intensity. "I haven't decided."

They ate and drank in silence until the water and cakes were consumed. Then, watching her until she raised her eyes to his, he said, "Your aunt has told me a great deal about you."

And me very little about you, Libby thought. She swallowed, uncomfortable with his admiring gaze. Surely he wasn't going to declare his affection so early in their acquaintance. What he'd said earlier echoed in her mind. *Here in the West we don't have time to stand on ceremony. Things are changing all the time.* She didn't like the direction their conversation was taking. "Robert," she said, "why are you so against the Wild West show? Can you not bury the past and forgive?"

His face changed in an instant, the way a fast-moving thundercloud turns day to night. He stood, dropped his napkin to the ground, and stepped away. He turned his back to her. For several seconds, he looked out on the landscape, the silence deafening. Then, without turning around, he said in a tight, controlled voice, "It's not the past I buried. It was my brother."

Libby stared in astonishment, able to see only his dejected profile. Men and women on both sides of the conflict had suffered and died, but the war was over. Both sides had sustained staggering losses, but people had to embrace what was left to them and accept one another.

It was right there in Omaha that a historic trial had taken place some years earlier. *Standing Bear v. Crook* had given Native Americans their citizenship. She found it ironic that people more American than any other should have to beg for a place to belong. Still, Robert had lost a brother. *Only seventeen,* she recalled and was touched with pity. "I am sorry, Robert."

"I shall not speak of this further," he declared, deadly quiet. Then, swiftly, his anger seemed to dissipate. His features became placid and genteel once more. He reached down to help her to her feet. "Forgive me if I spoiled what has been a most enjoyable morning." He drew her hand to his lips. "Now I must get you back. I trust you are rested."

They didn't speak again until they reached the homestead and rode the horses through the corral gate.

12

Cabot Falls, Vermont
Present Day

Sofia and Marla were ushered into Officer Quimby's office. It seemed to Sofia that he looked tired. More tired than she'd ever seen him before, though he offered them a quick smile.

He set down a half-finished cup of coffee and stood, dwarfing his desk. "I thought you might be by today," he said quietly.

The young policeman with the freckled Irish face had become a favorite of Sofia's. He'd been at the house for dinner several times. The kids loved hearing accounts of his activities. Even in the quiet community of Cabot Falls, things could get exciting.

Sofia noted the shadows around his eyes and the furrows in his forehead. A young artist had died tragically in the beloved community in which he had grown up.

Officer Quimby had done a stint in the U.S. Army right after high school but was medically discharged when his knees gave out due to an old football injury. One could detect a slight limp on occasion, usually in the cold or wet weather. But it didn't slow him down. Everyone knew he loved Cabot Falls and that in spite of ambitions to use his training in some more-sophisticated way, he'd likely never leave.

"Sorry about your show," he said, running a hand through his short-cropped hair. "I suppose it didn't help that we had to bring Homer in for questioning." He cleared his throat and gave Sofia a knowing look. Winifred Winslow's reputation was no secret.

"That won't be a problem," Marla said. "Rathbone Steele smoothed her ruffled feathers a little while ago. She's preening like a proud peacock and can't wait for the world to see her son's masterpieces."

Sofia shook her head. "Yes, and it looks like we'll have to go ahead with the show. The agency is holding us to the contract we signed."

"I've met your Mr. Steele," Officer Quimby said as he resumed his seat. He invited them to take the chairs near them with a gesture. "The man's alibi was sound, and he was cooperative enough. But he didn't seem too upset about his client." He raised one copper eyebrow. "From what I hear about the art world, an artist's popularity suddenly soars when he dies. Is that true?"

Sofia grimaced, remembering how Steele had whipped off the price tags, stating his intention to make adjustments now that Howahkan was no longer in the land of the living. "He's at the library as we speak, affixing new prices to the paintings," she said. "He wants to go ahead with the show as quickly as possible and work out financial details later with any next of kin who might have a claim to the artist's estate. According to Steele, there isn't much to quibble about. Howahkan was on the cusp of his career."

Officer Quimby looked down at a sheaf of papers on his desk. "We've tried to contact the sister—Willow June Hunt of Saratoga Springs, New York—but no luck so far." Officer Quimby's frown deepened. "I understand there was no love lost between her and her brother."

Sofia stiffened. The interest in Howahkan's sister seemed to go beyond confirming the identity of the body, which Steele had already done and which she herself could have done if asked.

Unable to keep the anxiety from her voice, Sofia said, "Is there something you're not telling us?" She waited while he tapped a pencil on his desk.

"There are a few things that don't exactly add up," he said slowly. "We know Mr. Blane was being treated for depression and that lethal amounts of an antidepressant were found in his system. And of course there's the note." He paused, his frown deepening. "On the surface, it appears the drugs were self-administered, but I'm not ready to sign off on this one as a suicide."

Sofia felt dark foreboding rising like a specter.

"We found the implements he probably used to inject the medication. But here's the thing, there are no fingerprints on the vial or the syringe."

The image of a discarded needle chilled Sofia, so she didn't immediately grasp the significance of his words. Then it dawned on her what Officer Quimby was suggesting. She studied the concern in his blue eyes. *Could the fingerprints have been smeared or compromised naturally somehow?*

Officer Quimby stroked his jaw. "I have to ask, would a man planning to do away with himself wipe off the vial after he drew the fatal dose? Or the syringe?" He raised an eyebrow. "Even if he had accidentally injected himself with more medication than he should take . . ." He shook his head as though he was dismissing the idea. "It's far more logical that someone was with our victim. Someone either tried to hide evidence or had a hand in his demise."

Sofia realized she was holding her breath. That Howahkan might have killed himself in the throes of depression was bad enough, but to think that someone could have murdered him . . . she couldn't quite wrap her mind around that. Steele's comments about Willow June Hunt throbbed in her memory. *Is it possible that his sister could hate him enough to kill him?* "So you believe

Howahkan's death was a homicide?" she asked tentatively.

"No," Officer Quimby said, shaking his head. "I'm simply viewing it as a suspicious death for now."

Sofia thought of the handsome artist in a hotel room in a strange town, suffering alone from whatever distress plagued him. *I can't do this anymore. I am sorry,* the note had read. "Ryan," she said, using his first name, which she usually reserved for social occasions, "could Marla and I have a look at his room?"

"Now, why am I not surprised?" His forehead furrowed. "We've gone over everything in that room pretty thoroughly. I don't think there's anything more to find, but I see no harm in indulging your curiosity." He paused, pushing back from his desk with a sigh. "Well, come on then."

They rode in the squad car toward the edge of town to the elegant Cabot Falls Inn. The brick building surrounded by lush foliage was definitely the go-to accommodation for anyone with an eye for style and comfort. The four-star inn boasted an elegant lobby, a modern elevator, and stylish rooms for dining or sleeping. Its dormer windows and hand-carved gingerbread gave it a personal feel, like a very large bed-and-breakfast.

Officer Quimby led the way to the second floor and then down the long corridor. The yellow police tape across the door easily identified room 217. She had checked the room out when she preregistered the artist because it was comfortable and roomy, befitting his status as an honored guest. She'd even ordered a lavish fruit basket, wrapped in cellophane and topped with a blue bow.

Officer Quimby nodded to the attendant, who opened the door with a key. He stepped back to allow Sofia and Marla to enter. It was eerily quiet and very like Sofia remembered it, except for the chalk outline on the carpet near the desk. Sofia avoided that area for the moment and took in the neatly made bed with the obligatory white service cards propped up on its pillows. The untouched fruit basket rested on a low table at the end of the bed.

"It looks like he didn't settle in at all," Marla said, her voice cracking slightly.

"No," Sofia agreed, glancing around the room. No suitcases or bags were there. They had probably been taken to the police station. Steele had said Howahkan planned to be in Cabot Falls only three days and would fly to Columbus right after the show closed. "Did he have a lot of luggage?" she asked Officer Quimby.

"One case with an assortment of Native American clothes—breeches, a suede coat, some jewelry, feathers. Probably stuff like on the ads promoting the art show. Of course there was the usual assortment of socks, underwear, and such. Guess he must have dressed up in traditional gear when he was on tour."

The stunning photo on the brochure filled Sofia's vision. She wondered how the artist felt about dressing in traditional Native American garb. She hoped he hadn't minded and had been proud of his heritage. Or had he felt he was being put "on display" like an endangered species in the zoo?

"We'll hold it for his family," Officer Quimby said, "if we find them. Steele told me his sister lives in Saratoga Springs."

"Apparently there's only the sister," Sofia said quietly, remembering Steele's pronouncement. *The poor boy was really quite alone in the world.* Upstate New York, where Steele said Willow June lived, was relatively near to Cabot Falls. She and her brother might have had an opportunity to visit, maybe to reconcile. Had this been in his mind when he'd accepted the showing?

How sad it was when family members became estranged. Life was lonely enough without letting your own family go. *What is Willow June's story?* Sofia wondered. *Did she take advantage of her brother's proximity to Saratoga Springs so she could confront him? Confront him—or something else?*

Sofia didn't like the trajectory of her thoughts and hurried to tell Officer Quimby everything she knew about the family. "According to his agent, Howahkan was driving the car in which both their parents were killed." She inhaled slowly and exhaled sharply. "Mr. Steele says the artist never got over it, and his sister never forgave him."

"We would very much like to talk to Ms. Hunt," Officer Quimby said, rubbing his jaw. They had moved together toward the marked carpet and stopped to take in the nearly artistic outline of Howahkan's body, which looked as though he had slept there.

No one spoke right away.

After a few seconds, Officer Quimby said, "We figure he was sitting at this desk and fell to the floor. The note and pen were on the desktop, as though he'd just written it."

Sofia shot Officer Quimby a questioning look.

"Yes, his prints were on the pen. The syringe and the vial were found on the floor over there." Officer Quimby pointed to two taped crosses marking the former locations of the items.

"Could the prints have been rubbed away when the vial and syringe rolled across the carpet?" Marla asked, peering closely at the marks.

"Not likely," Officer Quimby said firmly. "The items were entirely clean, not a smudge on them."

Sofia studied the light-colored carpet, which was a cool shade of ivory—unusually light for an institutional carpet, but then this was one of the more expensive rooms. It also had a rather thick pile. She bent to touch it and looked up at Officer Quimby. "Is it okay if I look around a bit?" She had no doubt the department had been thorough in its investigation, but something might have been overlooked. She brushed her hand lightly across the carpet.

"No problem," he said. "Everything's been dusted." He stepped aside. "I have a couple calls to make, but I'll be right outside if you need me. Go ahead and look to your heart's content."

An odd phrase, *heart's content.* There was nothing "content" about her heart at that moment. Nor had there been for Howahkan in this lonely room.

"I'll check the bathroom, though he may not have had time to use it," Marla said. "The towels look like the maid just hung them. They're still tied with fancy white ribbons."

On her knees, Sofia moved her fingers over the carpet's soft pile. She began close to the outline and expanded her search around the desk and chair. *A foolish waste of time,* she thought, and yet she continued, thinking how appropriate it was that she was on her knees. Howahkan's life had ended here, and he deserved a prayer.

She stretched her arm to reach under the desk, well beyond the space provided for the knees. Her fingers felt something. The object was smooth and hard and rolled easily into view. *A pearl!*

She stared at it for several seconds, wondering if she should pick it up. But she had already touched it, and no fingerprints could be detected on something so small anyway, could they? She picked it up and cupped it in the palm of her hand.

"Marla," she called.

Marla came out of the bathroom, sharp eyes questioning. "You found something?"

"It's a pearl. A single ivory-colored pearl, the same color as the carpet. I found it way under the desk." She rolled it around in her hand. "I guess ladies wear pearls these days, but I seldom see them. Maybe an older woman," she mused. "There's a slight rough spot here," she said, pointing.

Bending low over Sofia's kneeling form, Marla stared. "Could have come from a necklace or pin."

Had Howahkan received a female visitor? Willow June? Could the pearl belong to her? Had she been here and fought with him? Sofia's breath caught in her throat. *Had she lost it while struggling with the artist?* But there were no signs of struggle aside from a few roughed-up spots on the carpet that could have been made by Howahkan or one of the investigating officers.

"It could have been lost by a former occupant of the room," Sofia said.

"Might mean something," Marla said. "Or nothing. That pearl could have been there for a long time. It could belong to anyone."

Officer Quimby came through the door, frowning, cell phone in hand. He paused, narrowing his hazel eyes. "You found something?"

Sofia held the pearl out on her palm. "It was way under the desk," she said, noticing Officer Quimby's frown. "I'm sorry if I ruined any fingerprints it might have held."

He sighed and took it between his large fingers, drawing it close to his face to examine it. Marla peered over his shoulder and a small smile creased her lips. "You've found the pearl of great price."

"Probably not real," Sofia said. "Probably costume jewelry, and it could have come from anything."

Officer Quimby drew a small plastic evidence bag from his pocket and dropped the pearl into it. "Well, wherever it came from, it could be important, especially in light of what we've heard about the family dynamics." He gestured to his phone. "We know she's been here."

"Willow June Hunt?" asked Sofia in surprise.

He nodded. "Hospital says she asked to see the body. But she took off before anyone could detain her. I've sent someone over to get a statement from the morgue attendant." He thrust his jaw out in a determined gesture. "And we'll be on the lookout for her."

When Sofia and Marla stared in surprise, he added, "Pearl or no pearl, she's a person of interest."

13

Omaha, Nebraska
June 1885

"Teddy will have to take you in the buckboard," Aunt Tillie told Libby when they breakfasted together. "I need the carriage for the ladies' society meeting today. We'll be finalizing the plans for the mayor's ball to be held on Saturday." She gave Libby and Meg a look of mock severity. "I expect you girls to be there in your finest attire."

Libby nodded her assurance, pleased to have her aunt's permission to go with Teddy once more to the Wild West show. After all, Colonel Cody himself had invited them and given them free passes to the afternoon performance. Libby promised to "stick close to Teddy" and "mind her manners."

"I'm going to tell Teddy the good news," Libby told Meg. "I can't wait to see the 'Little Missie' Colonel Cody told us about."

"Do you think she's anything like that Miss Smith?" Meg asked.

"I hope not. The audience was impressed with her costume more than her marksmanship," Libby said, laughing. "Let's not mention her to Aunt Tillie."

On the way to the stable, Libby watched for anything moving in the tall grass that bordered the path. *There's more than one kind of snake to look out for,* she thought with a shiver. She didn't want to run into Hawk, though likely the offensive hired hand was already gone after Robert's verbal thrashing and threat to inform Aunt Tillie.

She found Teddy sketching with his charcoal, face intent upon the paper tacked onto a smooth piece of wood on his lap. He was so engrossed in his work that he didn't hear her come up behind him to peer over his shoulder.

He was drawing a girl in a fringed dress, who was dipping a clay waterpot into a stream. Her hair flowed long and sleek over her shoulder, and her head was turned slightly as if she had heard something that stopped her in the midst of her task. It was the same girl Libby had seen posted on the rough stable wall, a Native American girl with dark, soulful eyes and an expression of inscrutable sadness on her solemn lips.

"Her name is Chumani," he said, almost reverentially, after he sensed Libby's presence. "It means 'dewdrops.'" His freckled face reddened slightly.

Libby sat across from him on an overturned barrel in the tidy corner of the stable that was Teddy's small domain. He had told her he preferred this place near the horses where he could sketch without being interrupted. *Without men like Hawk to taunt him,* Libby thought.

"She's beautiful," she said as Teddy darkened the girl's hair with a few deft strokes. Libby was amazed that those chapped, work-worn hands could form such delicate lines and evoke such pathos. Yet in the arena, he was hard-riding and daring, an unusual mix of cowboy and artist indeed.

"Chumani travels with the Wild West troupe, her adoptive family," Teddy said. "Theirs is one of teepees in the village you see at the park." He added a stroke of his charcoal to the curve of the girl's moccasin. "Sitting Bull has two sons too. Their names are One Bull, who is adopted, and Crow Foot."

"She seems very troubled," Libby said, unable to take her eyes from the drawing.

Teddy pondered the picture. "Chumani worries about Sitting

Bull. If his people weren't so hungry and desperate, he would never have surrendered back in '81." He shook his head slowly. "Everyone was rounded up and forced to live on reservations. He was a great chief who fought hard for freedom. He wanted to be remembered as the last man of his tribe to surrender his rifle. But surrender he did. Chumani says he carries the burden like a stone on his heart."

Libby recalled the way the chief had responded to their attempt at kindness, and she understood Chumani's concern. Teddy knew a great deal about the Sioux. *And one girl in particular is special to him,* she mused. She wondered what this could mean for them.

Teddy smiled wryly. "At the Wild West show, the Indians can at least make some money of their own instead of living on government handouts."

She nodded, thinking of the colorful teepees at the arena. If the Wild West had to close, these families would once again be trundled off to the reservation. She watched Teddy work a shadow across the clay pot by Chumani's feet. It was quiet inside the stable, and Libby was content to sit quietly and watch Teddy work. A barn cat curled itself around her feet and purred softly. The scent of newly laid straw and the sound of the horses' nickering in the pasture calmed her. She might even have dozed if Teddy hadn't spoken.

"Did you enjoy your ride?" he asked idly, keeping his gaze on his work. "You and that Mr. Ealy?"

The way he said "that Mr. Ealy" brought her up short. She hesitated, studying Teddy. "We had an enjoyable ride around Aunt Tillie's property, which is really quite impressive." She paused, aware of Teddy's lightly creased forehead. "My aunt regards him highly. We're only friends, but of course she thinks he's the kind of man a girl should set her cap for. A gentleman of means."

Teddy's left eyebrow rose. He sat back a little, examined his composition, and resumed sketching. "I guess that was true once," he said. "I heard tell he lost everything and had to start all over. Business went under and his family was gone, except for his uncle here in Omaha."

Libby stared at his averted face, trying to reconcile what she was hearing. She had assumed that Robert was a man of means from his air of dignity and his expensive clothes. "How difficult for him," she murmured sympathetically. At the same time, she felt unnerved. Robert had made it sound as if he were doing the mayor a favor by coming to Omaha.

"He sidled up right quick to the wealthy folk hereabouts, like Mayor Quaid and Miz Primm," Teddy said after a few moments' silence.

Sidled up? She caught a look of distaste on Teddy's face. Was he saying that Robert was an opportunist? And if so, didn't people applaud that quality, especially in the West?

She recalled interactions she had witnessed between Robert and Mayor Quaid, first in Aunt Tillie's parlor and later at the Adelina Patti concert. Robert had been so angry with the mayor's introduction of Buffalo Bill that he had stormed out of the auditorium. Augustus Quaid may have sought Robert's expertise or assistance, but the two did not appear to be on the best of terms.

She regarded Teddy's face as he continued to sketch. Like her sister, it appeared that he was no fan of Robert's. "Are you trying to tell me something, Teddy?"

"Rumor is he had to leave Texas after a fight with someone on the town council." Teddy chewed his lip thoughtfully. "But it ain't none of my business. Still, I don't want you to get hurt."

Had Robert left Texas under a cloud of suspicion? Was he using Aunt Tillie and her friends to gain some advantage for himself? Or were those accounts merely rumors?

Teddy's words almost had a jealous ring to them, but she and Teddy didn't have that kind of relationship. He was too young, for one thing, and for another, anyone with eyes could see he was in love with Chumani.

The conversation clouded the pleasant peace of the morning. She was not in love with Robert, but she admitted to herself that she was flattered by his interest. But the anger in him had troubled her from their first conversation. She had deflected him from further intimacy when they sat under the cottonwood tree by asking about Cody's enterprise.

Robert, why are you so against the Wild West? Can you not bury the past and forgive?

It's not the past I buried. It was my brother.

She had felt pity for him in that moment. Pity and sadness over the terrors and memories of war that so obviously troubled him. Now she had to wonder, *Exactly who is Robert Ealy?*

Libby and Meg joined the crowd of spectators at Buffalo Bill's Wild West show and presented their free passes. They found seats in the canvas-covered grandstands that formed a horseshoe around the arena. Teddy was scheduled to "ride shotgun" on the Deadwood stagecoach in the absence of a performer who was under the weather. He cautioned them to wait for him so that when the last act was over, he could escort them back home.

The Cowboy Band struck up *The Star-Spangled Banner* and the show began with a band of Indians on horseback followed by cowboys waving their hats. As before, they came to a screeching halt in front of the stands.

Buffalo Bill again charged into the arena, crimson shirt and fringed jacket flaring, long hair cascading from his huge hat trimmed with silver studs. He pulled up at center stage to give his characteristic "Ready! Go!" and a kaleidoscopic maelstrom of color and sound broke the summer air.

The Cowboy Kid looked none the worse for wear as he rode with twin guns blazing, followed by vaqueros twirling lariats and more cowboys riding bucking broncos. A prairie schooner lumbered across the show lot, and a Pony Express rider changed horses with lightning speed. The combination rodeo-drama continued to the cheers and applause of the audience.

Midway through the program, right after Buffalo Bill enacted a duel with Yellow Hand, Annie Oakley—"the Peerless Lady Wing Shot"—was announced. Tripping in from the grandstand gangway was a demure five-foot girl with chestnut hair flowing down her back and a cowboy hat with a six-pointed star pinned to its turned-up brim. She wore a pair of pearl-buttoned leggings and a skirt that fell below her knees. The starched white collar of her loose-fitting blouse evoked a wholesome, well-pressed look—quite a contrast to Miss Smith.

Running to the center of the arena, the Peerless Lady Wing Shot took her place by a wooden table draped with a silken cover and laden with rifles and shotguns. A man, slightly shorter than average and sporting a handsome mustache, stood by to load the traps and release clay birds for her to shoot. According to Teddy, this was her partner and husband, Mr. Frank Butler.

The clay birds came singly at first, then in pairs, triplets, and finally, four at a time. She broke them in a whirl of motion, shooting with both hands and not missing a single clay bird Butler threw. Then came the glass balls heaved into the air. She took a pistol in her left hand and one in her right, fired them simultaneously, and broke target after target.

She proceeded to smash balls, first by firing a rifle held upside down over her head, then while lying on her back across a chair. The audience went wild. They were enchanted with her dramatic expressions, especially the humorous little kick she gave before ducking out of sight. Libby was charmed by the performance, and she was sorry when it was over.

She and Meg sat for nearly an hour waiting for Teddy to return. Just when they began to wonder if something dreadful had happened to him, he appeared, walking beside a beautiful dark-haired girl. She moved with her head down, eyes even sadder than Libby remembered them.

"Chumani," Teddy began softly, "these are my friends, Miss Elizabeth and Miss Margaret Carson."

The girl nodded gravely and stepped a little closer to Teddy. "Pleased to meet you," she said formally. Sitting Bull's adopted daughter likely had been educated in the white man's ways, perhaps at a mission school. Libby saw that she even had a little cross around her neck. Without correcting the formal address Teddy had employed, Libby smiled into the soulful eyes. "We, too, are pleased," she said warmly.

"Her pet is lost, and we were looking for him," Teddy explained. "He's very old and sometimes wanders off. We were going to Miss Annie Oakley's tent. She and Bright Eagle—that's Chumani's dog—they're friends, and we think he might have gone to her tent. Do you mind going along with us?" Teddy's eyes were eager. "I'd like you to meet Miss Annie."

Libby tried not to show her excitement at the opportunity to meet the charming sharpshooter. "By all means," she said. "Meg and I would like to help and meet Miss Oakley."

Together they dodged the performers who were busy putting away animals, props, and other paraphernalia after the show. Shards of broken glass and debris from exploded clay pigeons were being swept away. As they approached the tenting area, Libby saw people talking in small groups, voices low, faces clouded. Had something else happened to cause concern?

Teddy stopped at a midsize tent with one side completely open to reveal canvas walls lined with rifles. On the floor of the tent was a woven rug on which a rocking chair was poised, still moving, as though someone had recently risen from it. Beside it was a basket with colorful fabrics and a small table topped with a vase of flowers.

"She makes all her own costumes," Teddy whispered. "Right there in that rocking chair."

Libby looked inside at the neat interior. *A sharpshooter who is also a seamstress!*

She spied Annie with a group of men huddled together at a nearby tent. One of them was a dignified man wearing both a business suit and a grave expression.

"That's Mr. Salsbury, the business manager," Teddy said in a surprised whisper. He stopped short and gestured for them all to stay back until the manager and the others had finished their conversation and moved off.

The young sharpshooter stood motionless as the men departed. She was still dressed in her costume, with embroidered flowers down each side of her fringed skirt. Under the felt hat, her long chestnut hair was caught in two portions and draped over her shoulders. Every inch a Victorian lady, she looked out at them with gentle brown eyes, gentle but clearly troubled.

Seeing Chumani, Annie Oakley went to her, then turned questioning eyes on Teddy.

"These are my friends, visitors at Miz Primm's homestead," he said. "They came to help us look for Bright Eagle." He studied the face of the young performer. "Is everything all right, Miss Annie?" Teddy asked.

Annie nodded to Libby and Meg politely, then answered in a soft, well-modulated voice. "I'm afraid things are not all right, Teddy. Not all right at all. The entire proceeds of this week's earnings have disappeared." Her brown eyes widened, her voice heavy with sadness. "There is no money to run the Wild West show."

14

Cabot Falls, Vermont
Present Day

"I'm so sorry about the art show," Gina said, making a steeple of her fingers.

Sofia found her sister waiting for her when she got home in the late afternoon after finding the pearl at the Cabot Falls Inn. She'd dropped in unannounced; it was clear that Gina was not only curious but also sympathetic concerning the recent events in her sister's life.

"Rosa wanted to come too, but she couldn't get away today," Gina said, cocking her sleek auburn head to one side.

They hadn't talked since the celebration of Nonna's birthday, an evening that hadn't ended well after the discovery of the hole in the quilt.

"We both feel bad about the other night," Gina said sheepishly. "We didn't think before we blamed you for something that probably wasn't your fault at all."

"No," Sofia said. "It's all right. We were all upset. We couldn't help but be. But I have something to tell you about that later when it's not so crazy." Sofia kicked off her shoes as Matthew and Luke came running into the foyer to greet her. They didn't always do that, and it touched her now. *I'm so grateful to have these wonderful people who care about me.*

"I got up to the next level. I'm at eleven now," Luke said,

indicating his latest achievement as the family's computer game champion. After a brief hug, he went back to make his next digital conquest. Matthew, the youngest, waved a test paper under her nose. It had a big red A at its top.

"Oh, that's terrific. I'm so proud of you," she said, moving toward the kitchen with Gina at her side. Wynter was preparing a salad and Jim was spooning mounds of spaghetti into a large bowl. "You guys are great," she said, beaming at Vanessa, who had likely initiated and directed the meal prep.

Jim gave her shoulders an extra squeeze when he seated her at the table, then pushed Gina's chair in as well. Sofia had talked to her husband earlier in the afternoon and filled him in on the developments of Howahkan's case. Jim had promised that he and the kids would take care of dinner. She smiled up at him and saw that he looked tired. Or maybe it was worry creasing his forehead.

"You be careful," he had told her when she described Officer Quimby's suspicions of foul play. "If there's some nutcase out there . . ."

But she quickly had allayed his fears. As far as anyone could tell, Howahkan was the only target, and it was too late for him to be careful.

Jim didn't resent her penchant for mystery, and he applauded her keen observation skills, but she knew he worried about her. She gave him a fond smile and passed him the rolls. "Thanks for filling in for me," she said to everyone in general when they were seated around the table. "It's been a roller coaster these last few days, and I've left you to fend for yourselves."

"What are you going to do about the show?" Gina asked, helping herself to a second roll.

"We're going to go ahead with it. We'd hoped to begin on Thursday and run through Saturday. But we've decided to begin with a reception to open the show this evening and run through tomorrow night. It's not ideal, but it's the best solution we could come up with under the circumstances."

"Fine thing, the artist deciding to commit suicide right here in Cabot Falls," Gina said.

Sofia shot her sister a stern look. "The children," she said.

"Come on, Mom," Wynter blurted out in true Wynter form, complete with eye rolling. "Everyone's talking about it. And we're not babies. People kill themselves all the time."

"They do not kill themselves all the time," she countered. "And besides, the police aren't sure that's what happened. They're still investigating."

"You mean somebody murdered him?" Luke asked, stopping in midchew, his mouth full of spaghetti.

"We don't know that either," Sofia said. "And don't talk with your mouth full." Then, more softly, she added, "It could have been an accident. But we should all be thinking of his loved ones at this time and show the proper respect." Grimly she recalled Rathbone Steele's words. *His only family would be happy to be rid of him.*

"Your mom's right. This is hardly dinner conversation." Jim weighed in with a sharp glance in Wynter's direction. "I know we've all been concerned about the art show. Your mom has worked hard to make it a success. It's going on as planned with only a slight delay. As for the investigation, we'll leave that to the police." His eyes came to rest on Sofia as he finished his sentence.

Sofia had been able to think of little else since finding the pearl in Howahkan's hotel room. There would be little respect and severe consequences for Willow June if it was determined that the pearl belonged to her. Ryan Quimby had said that Howahkan's estranged sister had been in town but had left before she could be detained.

Did she know the police were looking for her? They didn't have enough evidence to arrest her, but along with everyone else connected with the art show, she was considered "a person of interest." Had she run away after satisfying herself that her brother was really dead? Sofia shivered and couldn't help hoping that the artist's sister could prove she hadn't been in Cabot Falls the night Howahkan died. Still, how had Willow June known to come to Cabot Falls? Officer Quimby said he hadn't been able to locate her.

"She could have found Howahkan's itinerary on his website," Marla had said. Sofia knew that Steele and Steele Agency maintained the artist's website. In fact, the committee had first learned about his work through that website. Maybe Willow June kept track of her brother's showings. *Could it be she was waiting for him when he got to the inn?*

Sofia forced herself to put the mystery on the back burner of her mind and to concentrate on her family's recent activities. Vanessa had submitted one of her dress designs to a needlecraft magazine contest. Wynter's sophomore soccer team had made it to the divisional finals. The boys debated the merits of the latest animated movie they'd seen.

When dinner was over, the children cleared the table, and Jim left Gina and Sofia to enjoy conversation in the four-season room that adjoined the kitchen, knowing that Sofia would have to leave soon for the opening reception at the art show.

"I love this room," Gina said, choosing one of the white wicker chairs padded with gingham fabric cushions. She propped her feet on a matching ottoman. "It's so cozy, but what I like best is that fabulous view." She stretched an arm toward the window that spanned nearly the entire wall. "It's the perfect place for you and your painter friends."

"Jim's handiwork," Sofia said proudly, taking the chair across from her sister. "It's my favorite room too. I've spent a lot of happy hours here."

Gina took a long breath and let it out slowly. "I bet those gorgeous woods give you a lot of inspiration. Look at the way the light filters through the trees and casts those beautiful shadows. It's like a slow dance." Gina's blue eyes were alight with wonder.

"You sound more like a poet than a microbiology professor," Sofia said. "But you always were full of surprises, big sister." She joined Gina in admiration of the spectacular view, and the two sat companionably while their coffee cooled on the low table.

"You were preoccupied all through dinner," Gina said. "Is it the quilt that's got you down or the artist who died?"

Sofia frowned, realizing she hadn't been as attentive as she'd thought at dinner. She picked up the diary that she had brought down earlier from her bedroom trunk. She turned it over in her hands meditatively. "Actually, it's both," she said.

"Really, it's not your fault," Gina interrupted. "Things happen in spite of our best intentions. We know you take good care of Nonna's wonderful quilt. You've got enough on your plate to worry about without us getting on your case."

Sofia shook her head. "That's not it. I haven't had time to investigate how that hole got there. These last few days have kept me running through the day and tossing and turning at night. I haven't had a chance to think about the quilt. But last night I looked up the entry for that lavender swatch and discovered the most amazing set of coincidences."

Gina moved her legs from the ottoman and leaned forward, narrowing her eyes. Her auburn hair curved around her face.

"We knew that Nonna had a friend whose grandaunts spent some time out West and even got to meet Buffalo Bill," Sofia said.

"Sure," Gina said, "I remember her talking about two sisters from Massachusetts who went to Nebraska."

Sofia opened the diary to the page where she had left off reading the night before. "The story is really exciting," Sofia said. "I haven't finished it, but I'm still mulling over something that really floors me."

Gina got up and pulled her chair closer to her sister, craning her short neck to see the handwritten diary.

"The girls were Libby and Meg Carson, fresh from finishing school when they went to visit their aunt, who was a proper Victorian lady with plans for her nieces to mingle in the best society." Sofia bowed over the page and paraphrased. "They were enthralled with what they'd heard about 'cowboys and Indians.' They even found a Native American along the road on their very first night in Nebraska. He was injured and the girls tried to help, using a shawl to clean his wounds. Later they got to see a real Wild West show run by Buffalo Bill, history's most famous scout and Pony Express rider."

"Intriguing, but what is the coincidence you mentioned?" Gina asked.

"See this name here?" Sofia pointed gently, careful not to crease the page.

"Theodore Blane?" Gina asked.

"Teddy. He was a young cowboy who took care of the horses on the ranch the girls were visiting. He also worked for Buffalo Bill and brought the girls to see the show. He also liked to sketch western scenes." She paused and shifted the diary. "At first I didn't make the connection. The artist Howahkan—our artist who died—his real name is Skylar Blane. The biographical information on him says he was the great-grandson of a marginally known sketch artist named Theodore Blane."

"You think they're related?" Gina was a stickler for good scholarship and never took anything at face value.

"That's when I stopped reading the diary and got on the

computer," Sofia said. She had stayed up half the night researching and confirming Howahkan's genealogy. "The professional bio says Theodore married a Sioux princess. One of the children born to them became the grandparent of Skylar and Willow June."

Gina looked at her sister, her eyes wide. "Wow," she said at length, "that *is* a coincidence. Did he know?"

"I never had a chance to talk to him about it," Sofia replied, feeling grief well up. Discovering Nonna's connection to Howahkan had made the tragedy of the dead artist and his estranged sister personal somehow. And sadly, she would never have the opportunity to share this common link with Skylar Blane.

"You said he wasn't very communicative," Gina mused.

"And deeply sad. Both his parents were killed in a car accident. Howahkan was driving. His agent, who claims he was the artist's only real friend, said Willow June blamed her brother all these years. He said that she would be glad he was dead." She recalled how easily Rathbone Steele had cast Howahkan's sister in an ugly light.

"Oh, Sofia, that's awful! And the police aren't satisfied that he killed himself?" Gina exclaimed.

"That's right, because of the lack of fingerprints on the vial and syringe. And then there's what happened today when Marla and I went to view the crime scene."

"You went to the crime scene? Does Jim know?"

"Yes, he knows," she said quickly. *But I didn't tell him until after I'd gone to the hotel.*

"What happened?" Gina pressed.

"We found a pearl." She shrugged. "It could have been there a long time. It was way under the desk. But that was where Howahkan had been sitting when he fell. It could have come from whoever was in the room at the time of death." Sofia drew in her breath.

"And you think maybe his sister was there?" Gina asked.

"She was at least at the morgue, asking to see his body. The police are looking for her to find out if she was at the hotel when he died," Sofia said. "Nonna would be so sad if she knew what had happened to the descendants of her friends from the diary."

The two were quiet for a while until Gina shook her head slowly. "I don't know how you get yourself involved in these things. You were always the curious one." She gave her sister a wondering but decidedly fond look. "But remember, curiosity killed the cat."

"Now you sound like Jim," Sofia said. "Anyway, when this show is over, I'm going to read the rest of the story. Then I'll see what can be done to repair the hole in the quilt."

"Be careful, sister. You're the only pearl we care about."

But even as she returned her sister's warm glance, something preyed on her mind. Something about that pearl. She got up and walked slowly toward the wide window where night was settling around the dark trees like a down comforter. It wasn't only women who wore pearls. And like an arrow piercing her mind, she had a vision of Rathbone Steele's gold cuff links with little white stones. *Pearls.*

15

Omaha, Nebraska
June 1885

Teddy drove the buckboard up the winding driveway toward the house, urging the horses to move faster. "I hope Miz Primm won't be too angry," he said. "It's late, and you missed supper. I'm sorry I couldn't get you back in time."

"We'll explain what happened," Libby said with a reassuring smile. Aunt Tillie was overly class conscious and a stickler for punctuality, but she had a big heart. Beyond that, she was nobody's fool.

Libby had hated leaving Annie Oakley and the dispirited Chumani at the Wild West show. Finding Chumani's aged dog, Bright Eagle, was a concern, but it paled in comparison to the serious loss of revenue that could mean the demise of Buffalo Bill's show. Libby recalled the group of stern faces around Annie Oakley's tent and Annie's grave news that the money to run the Wild West performances was gone.

"What do you think will happen now?" Meg asked, hazel eyes wide.

"The sheriff and his deputies will search every tent on the grounds," Teddy said. "They'll question everyone connected with the show." He exhaled a long breath. "But if we can't get the money back, we're sunk."

Libby chewed the inside of her cheek, thinking hard. "I want to help if I can." *Who has a motive for this attack on the Wild West show? Is the robbery connected with the assaults?* She looked from Meg to Teddy as they sat in the buckboard. "We could do some looking around, talk to some of the performers and see what we can find out."

"It had to be someone connected with the show," Meg said. "An outsider couldn't have known where the receipts were kept or how to make off with them without getting caught."

"Or someone who used to be connected," Libby said, her mind immediately zeroing in on the offensive Hawk, whom Cody had fired. *The perpetrator has to be someone with inside knowledge.* "Has Hawk ever come around the park since he got fired?" she asked Teddy.

He shrugged. "Not that I know of."

"He's about to be fired again," Libby said. "This time by Aunt Tillie, if Robert has anything to say about it." Briefly she related finding Hawk smoking in the stables and Robert's threat to inform Aunt Tillie.

Teddy's forehead wrinkled. "Mr. Ealy don't have much good to say about any of us workers, but he always chooses Hawk to handle his carriage when he comes to the ranch."

Robert chooses Hawk? Even though it's Teddy who has responsibility for the horses?

Teddy hopped down from the buckboard to hand Libby and Meg down. "I'm going to ride Prince out to the arena tomorrow, ask some questions, see if I can help," Teddy said. "I figure I'll go about midmorning when I've finished here."

"We want to go with you," Libby announced decisively. Her heart raced with anticipation. The park wasn't far, and Aunt Tillie would understand, she hoped. "Have some horses saddled for us. We'll be ready."

It wasn't until she and Meg got down from the buckboard

that Libby glimpsed an unfamiliar carriage drawn up under a tree on the west side of the homestead. Aunt Tillie had guests. *Maybe whoever it is won't stay long,* she thought hopefully. She was hungry and eager for some time to be alone and think.

"Where have you girls been?" Aunt Tillie said as she stepped out onto the stone porch. "It's nearly seven o'clock." She looked less angry than worried. Her salt-and-pepper hair had strayed from its tethering bun, and her cheeks were flushed. She narrowed her eyes at Teddy's disappearing form and glanced from Libby to Meg as though she could confirm their well-being with a look. "Teddy should have had you back hours ago, when dinner was served."

"We're very sorry to be late, but we're quite all right," Libby began to explain. "There was some trouble at the Wild West show."

Tillie held her arms out to usher them inside, nodding and gesturing with animated brown eyes. "Never mind that now." Lowering her voice, she jerked her head toward the parlor. "We have company. Come in and put your things away."

Libby glanced through the open door to see Robert Ealy sitting in Tillie's best parlor chair, long legs stretched out in front of him, arms crossed over his waistcoat. *Oh no. Not now.* Fragments of Teddy's less-than-complimentary mention of "that Robert Ealy" flashed through her mind as she hung her bonnet and wrap in the outer hall.

"Mr. Ealy and I were having tea," Tillie said, fussing with the too-long ribbons on Meg's bonnet. "Just scones, but I'll have Greta bring some sandwiches in for you. Dreadful that you've missed your supper. I declare, you must be famished." Aunt Tillie had a fondness for talk, but when she was nervous—and she was almost always nervous in the presence of company she deemed important—she rambled on, hardly pausing for breath.

"We're sorry to worry you," Libby said, annoyed with Robert for sidling up to Aunt Tillie. "Something happened today that kept Teddy longer than usual."

"Again? Well . . . never mind now," she commanded, tucking wisps of stray hair back from her perspiring forehead. "Go wash up and come in as soon as you're presentable. Greta brought fresh water for the basin. Look at the dust on your skirts and shoes." With that, Aunt Tillie straightened her shoulders and disappeared into the parlor, still talking.

Libby changed her dress and shoes after washing her hands and face. How could she calmly socialize with Robert Ealy after what she had heard? There were things she needed to know, but how was she to find out the truth? Was it right to trust Teddy's opinion of Robert? Even he had said the stories were rumor.

She cast a worried glance at Meg as she finished wiping dust from her shoes. "I don't begrudge Robert visiting Aunt Tillie, but why must he be here tonight?" Maybe he was here to give Aunt Tillie a report that would dispense of the odious Hawk?

Meg combed through her fine blond hair and twisted it again into a neat chignon. "It's likely you he's come for," she said mildly, still wearing a frown. "Are you not glad to see him?"

Libby studied her sister's face until Meg dropped her eyes. "Meg, what is it you don't like about Robert?"

"I haven't said I dislike him."

"In a hundred ways, you have." Libby shook her head in confusion. "Meg darling, if you know something, you need to tell me."

"I don't *know* anything, but Sonja says . . . that is, her mother . . ." She bit her lip, looking miserable. "I know you like him. He's very gallant and—"

"What?" Libby pressed. "What does Sonja say?"

"Greta hears things. She's been with Aunt Tillie for months

now." She fussed with her hair and didn't make eye contact with her sister. "She doesn't like the way he plays up to Aunt Tillie. And she's heard him and his uncle arguing. Robert wanted to foreclose on some property the bank owns, but the mayor refused to authorize it. She says Robert got very angry. A man who can't keep his temper can't be trusted."

Libby stared into her sister's hazel eyes, her mind whirling with conflicting thoughts. She'd been taught not to listen to gossip. She knew almost nothing about Greta, and she'd only known Teddy for a few days. Yet both of them distrusted Robert Ealy. Could he have anything to do with what was happening to Cody? Was he so angry over the death of his brother and Buffalo Bill's hiring of Indians that he would try to ruin him?

She took Meg's arm. "We'd better get in or Aunt Tillie will be coming after us," she said very quietly. "And don't worry. Mr. Ealy and I have shared only friendly conversation."

"There you are, darlings," Aunt Tillie crooned when they stepped inside the parlor.

Robert immediately stood. Elegant in dark trousers and jacket, he bowed to each of them in turn but fixed his gaze on Libby, the blue of his silken cravat reflected in his eyes. "Your aunt kindly said I might wait so as to spend a few minutes with you. I understand you've had a long day."

Libby gave a slight curtsy and took one of the chairs across from her aunt and Robert. Meg joined Aunt Tillie on the small settee with its crocheted antimacassar. Greta quickly brought a tray and set it on the low table before them. Choosing a sandwich from the tray and stirring sugar into her tea gave Libby a chance to formulate a response.

"Thank you," Libby said. "We have indeed had an interesting day. We met a wonderful performer at the Wild West show, Miss Annie Oakley." She glanced at Robert, but his expression remained fixed. "You remember," she pressed. "Buffalo Bill Cody announced it at the concert you so kindly arranged for us to attend."

Robert gave a little nod to show that he was listening, but a tiny vein in his temple began to pulsate.

"Another exhibition shooter," Aunt Tillie said without rancor. "They're quite the thing in circuses and such, and the newspapers are full of the feats of Mr. Bogardus and Mr. Carver. Some of those fancy shooters employ women in their acts."

"Annie Oakley is a performer in her own right," Libby said with a generous smile. "Mr. Butler throws the glass balls and clay pigeons, but Annie shoots them and doesn't miss a one. She is really quite wonderful and very ladylike."

"And she sews and embroiders," Meg said. "She makes all of her own costumes. We saw her tent and the rocking chair where she sews when she's not performing."

"Sitting Bull likes her so much that he adopted her," Libby added. "He calls her 'Little Sure Shot.' Of course, Buffalo Bill calls her 'Little Missie.'" She glanced at Robert from the corner of her eye to see how he was taking all this talk of the Wild West. Knowing his dislike of Indians, she was aware that she might be antagonizing him, but something goaded her on. "She's very young and barely five feet tall, but I've never seen anyone able to shoot like her."

Aunt Tillie squirmed and knotted her fingers in her lap. She had been at the auditorium the night Robert stormed out after Buffalo Bill's announcement. She had to know his feelings about the western show so many in town were praising. She blushed slightly and leaned forward. "May I give you another scone or a sandwich, Robert?"

Robert appeared startled. "Oh no, thank you. I've had quite enough," he said, his lips forming a forced smile.

Quite enough tea and scones or quite enough talk of Buffalo Bill Cody? Libby wondered.

"I have kept you long enough as well," Robert said. "I should be going." He stood, touching a hand to his cravat that was affixed with a handsome trinket. "Always a pleasure to see you, Mrs. Primm," he said formally. He put out a hand as she began to rise, favoring her with an indulgent smile. "No, don't trouble yourself to get up."

Tillie settled back down. "You will be coming to the mayor's ball on Saturday, won't you, Robert? The ladies' society has planned a magnificent fete truly worthy of your excellent uncle. Of course, we'll all be there." She glanced briefly at Meg and Libby before looking back at Robert. "Indeed, the whole city of Omaha will want to turn out for such a grand occasion."

He bowed graciously to Aunt Tillie. "Of course," he said, nodding and buttoning his jacket. Turning to Libby, he bowed once more and cleared his throat. "I wonder, Miss Elizabeth, if you would get my hat."

She rose hesitantly. "Of course," she managed. She set her teacup down on the enameled tray and went into the hall where the hat rack stood near the door. She lifted Robert's derby, turned to give it to him, and nearly collided with him. He was standing so close that she could feel the heat of his body. She stepped away in surprise, aware of her quickened heartbeat.

"Libby," he said huskily, "I was hoping for an opportunity to speak to you." Before she could draw them away, he clasped the fingers of her hand along with the hat she held out to him. His eyes warmed from ice-blue to a penetrating green. "You must know how I value your company. Would you do me the honor of taking a brief turn outside with me?"

There was something so intrusive about that husky voice, those ever-changing eyes. She had felt only sadness for him before.

Now she was suddenly frightened. What had changed? Why was her heart racing? Because of rumors repeated by a hired hand and an impressionable maid? "I'm so sorry, Robert," she heard herself say. "I'm very tired, and I have the beginnings of a headache. I'm afraid I must decline."

He stepped back slightly, as though caught off guard. "Of course. I understand." He fumbled with his derby, turning it around before adding, "I trust a good night's rest will restore you to health." He smiled, holding her gaze. "And I hope you'll save a dance for me on Saturday." He placed his hat on his head and ducked out the door.

She stood in the outer hall for a long, confused moment before returning to the parlor.

"Are you quite all right, darling?" Aunt Tillie asked, cocking her head a little. "I thought you and Robert might—"

"I'm really too tired for a stroll tonight, Aunt Tillie. I'm sure he'll understand." She hesitated and sat down on the settee. "Tell me about Robert," she said quietly when she was settled. "I mean, where does he come from? What did he do before he came to Nebraska?"

"Why, he is Mayor Quaid's nephew, a fine gentleman who served with our troops and now works with his uncle." She looked at Libby with a puzzled expression. "Is there a problem?" Her brown eyes flashed.

"No no," Libby assured her. "Sometimes he seems a bit brusque. I thought maybe it was a regional mannerism." She couldn't explain without sounding like a tattling child. And besides, now she did have a headache. With great effort, she forced a smile. "Wonderful scones and sandwiches. Thank you, Aunt Tillie."

"Meg has been telling me about a theft at the Wild West show," Tillie said tentatively.

"It's true. The entire week's proceeds were taken from the

business office. Teddy fears it will be the end of the show here in Omaha. A lot of people will be left out in the cold if the money isn't recovered. People who depend on Cody's western show." She paused, watching Aunt Tillie's concerned expression. After a rare few minutes of silence, she said, "Meg and I would like to ride out to the show tomorrow with Teddy. We want to see if there's something we can do to help."

Tillie frowned. "Robert thinks I ought not to give such liberties to my hired hands. He says Teddy is not completely reliable."

"Have you ever found him to be unreliable, Aunt Tillie?" Libby asked. Then quickly she added, "He has been the soul of discretion and certainly capable. I told you about the rattlesnake and how Teddy saved us."

"Yes, and I am grateful that he was watching out for you. I'm sure he's a respectable sort. It's just . . ." But Aunt Tillie wouldn't say what *it* was. Instead she put an arm around each of them. "Do be careful. If someone is perpetrating trouble out there at the arena, I certainly don't want you in harm's way."

"We'll be very careful, Aunt Tillie."

"But I want you home early," she said sternly. "No later than five o'clock supper."

16

Cabot Falls, Vermont
Present Day

*S*leep didn't come easy for Sofia from the time her head hit
the pillow late Friday night. Skylar Blane, Willow June, Rathbone
Steele, and Homer Winslow all tossed and turned in her mind as
she tried to rest. In and out of twisted dreams, they plagued her
with their haunting faces. Who had been with Howahkan the
night he died? And what had really happened in that hotel room?

Last night's opening had gone well. They had held a simple
reception to launch the event. No doubt the news of the artist's
sudden demise had fueled the interest of Cabot Falls's citizens.
But quite apart from being attracted by the notoriety, they were
culturally alert and eager to embrace new expressions in art. She'd
been weary by the end of the night.

Since Saturday was going to demand her energy from morning
until night, she'd gone to bed without reading any more from
Nonna's diary. However intrigued she was by Libby and Meg
Carson and the odd connection between them and Skylar Blane,
she had to be fresh for Saturday's show.

She woke early, knowing she was to meet the rest of the
committee members at the library by eight thirty in advance of
the ten o'clock start time. The sun was shining. *A good omen*,
she thought as she grabbed orange juice and a day-old pecan
roll. Jim and the kids were on their own again this morning, but

when this was all over, she'd make her family the best breakfast they'd ever had.

"We'll be there, honey," Jim said, "soon as the kids get ready. Likely not for an hour or so, but you'll be too busy with crowd control to even notice we're not there."

"Not a chance," she said wrapping her arms around his neck. "I'll always miss you."

He returned her kiss gently. "Maybe we can snatch you away for a quick sandwich at noon." A shadow crossed his face, and his blue eyes narrowed. "You will be careful, right? I think there's something not quite right about that art agency."

"I promise," she said.

"I tried to find out about Steele and Steele Agency, but the place doesn't even have a decent website," Jim continued. "One link shows Rathbone Steele, art collector and agent, but no official firm. Doesn't that seem odd to you?" He pressed his lips together.

Why hadn't she checked more deeply into the agency representing the Native American artist? They had all been so intrigued by Howahkan's bio. A lot of independent agents made their livings managing the talents of others; there was nothing strange about that.

She hadn't considered Rathbone Steele as a suspect. After all, he hadn't even been in town on Wednesday night when Howahkan died. He'd arrived in a rental car that he picked up at the airport on Thursday. Officer Quimby had checked with the airlines to confirm Steele's ticket, which he had produced upon being questioned. Steele was a pompous, greedy man but surely not dangerous.

She sighed as she placed her glass on the counter. "In a couple of days it'll all be over." She meant to reassure him as she waved goodbye, but would it really be all over? *How will it end?*

At the library, she joined Marla and the other volunteers to prepare for the day's activities. The painting of the Native American maiden by the water had been moved to a large easel in the main exhibition area as a way to draw the crowds in. By any estimation, the huge work was stunning. Sofia found herself touched again by its beauty and pathos. The sun-bronzed face, though painted in profile, revealed high cheekbones and a solemn, bow-shaped mouth. She was pulled through the painting from the shining black hair falling over delicate shoulders to the graceful angle of her body as she bent to fill her waterpot.

Rathbone Steele would stand in for Howahkan and exhibit his paintings. He had ordered that a desk be placed in the reading room for his use as well as a long table on which he intended to display Native American artifacts supposedly belonging to the artist. She recalled how he had greeted town officials the evening before, bowing deferentially to the mayor and his wife and in turn to Winifred Winslow.

Today Steele was dressed in a well-cut designer suit and an expensive silk tie in a Navajo-style print. His curly gray hair, trimmed neatly around his ears, was bushy in back and fringed the collar of his suit. Sofia's eyes went to his cufflinks, silver with small red jewels. He nodded to her and went into the reading room, quickly detaching himself from the thickening crowd.

Wearing her hostess badge, Sofia mingled with the guests, exchanging greetings with those she knew, answering questions, and handing out coupons provided by local businesses. Some visitors took advantage of the library's comfortable chairs, which had been arranged in small groupings to allow for quiet meditation.

She circled the perimeter several times, making herself available to guests of the show. A little later in the morning, Sofia noticed a woman, possibly in her late thirties or early forties, standing alone near the painting of the Native American maiden.

She had been there without moving for several minutes, staring through lightly tinted sunglasses. Of medium height and very thin build, she wore a sleeveless black dress and slingback pumps. Her jet-black hair was drawn into a large chignon at the base of her slender neck. The whole effect made Sofia think of the perennially popular Audrey Hepburn.

The woman did not acknowledge Sofia's smile of greeting, but remained poised near the easel. When Sofia made the circle around the library again, she was still there, head slightly bent, dabbing at the corner of her eye behind the glasses. Sofia's heart went out to her. But then perhaps she was simply touched by what she saw. People had varying responses to fine art.

But suddenly Sofia was arrested by the woman's profile. She looked from her to the painting and back again, and her breath caught in her throat. The resemblance was unmistakable.

Stopping alongside her, Sofia asked quietly, "Are you familiar with Howahkan's work?"

Startled, she took a step back. "No. I . . ." She sniffed, touching a tissue to her nose. "That is, I . . ." She ringed delicately arched lips with her tongue and swallowed as though she were thirsty, but she didn't finish her statement.

Sofia's mind was transported back to Wednesday night, to a silent and somber Howahkan sitting next to her in the car. Something in the arch of this woman's cheek and the set of her jaw was very like his. She peered through the glasses to see that the woman's eyes were red-rimmed and puffy. Could this be Howahkan's sister, Willow June?

Sofia touched her arm lightly. "I'm sorry about your brother," she said hesitantly.

The eyes widened in shocked surprise. She appeared poised to run but then wilted, bending forward and hugging her arms at her waist.

"Come," Sofia whispered. "We can sit over here." She led her to an unpopulated corner with two overstuffed chairs near a window. They sat without speaking while Willow June composed herself.

Willow June shook her head from side to side. "I don't understand," she said in a small voice. Her eyes roamed left and right, touching Sofia's only briefly. "When I left him, I thought . . ."

Sofia waited. Was she addressing the tragedy that had estranged the two? "Do you mean when you were separated? After the accident?"

Willow June's mouth opened. She shook her head gravely, then stared into space. "When I left him three days ago at the hotel."

Three days ago? Sofia's heart thudded. She *had* been at Howahkan's hotel three days ago. Had the small white pearl she'd found in the carpet belonged to her? What had this beautiful young woman done? "Willow June, do you know that the police are looking for you?"

She didn't seem rattled by Sofia's bold question and continued looking off into some distance Sofia couldn't reach. "I told him I was sorry for all the years that had come between us. I finally forgave him for what happened." She paused again and clutched the tissue in her slender fingers. "I wasted so much time." Suddenly she faced Sofia directly, her face twisted with grief. "Why would he do this now? Why?"

Sofia stared in amazement. Willow June believed her brother had killed himself.

Dropping her head into her hands, the woman wept softly. Eventually she shook the tears away, blinking hard. "The night our parents died, Sky was drunk. I blamed him. I blamed him for a long time, but then he told me about his depression. I guess he couldn't forgive himself either. I tried to keep track of him once I realized how wrong it was to keep on making him pay for what happened. Finally I decided to go to see him, to tell him I was sorry." She broke off and worked to steady herself. "We planned to have breakfast the next morning. That's when I heard."

Sofia's mind raced to analyze what might have occurred. The police hadn't been able to locate Willow June in her hometown because she had already come to Cabot Falls. She had seen Howahkan in the hotel and left, planning to have breakfast with him on Thursday morning.

If he had reconciled with his sister, would he have killed himself? That made no sense. Nor did it make sense that Willow June had been responsible for his death. She would hardly hang around, waiting for the police to arrest her. Obviously, Willow June believed Howahkan had killed himself. "I'm so sorry," Sofia said gently. "Why do you think he did it?"

"He hated what he was doing, traveling all over the country and being put on display. That man made a mockery of our Native American heritage, dressing him up like some sort of sideshow act."

"Do you mean his agent?" Sofia asked. Her eyes went automatically across the large expanse to the enclosed room where Rathbone Steele was waxing eloquent and enticing viewers to buy the departed artist's works, which he claimed would eventually become invaluable.

Willow June bit her lip. Her eyes darkened. "Yes. He completely controlled him. He pretended to help my brother." She paused as though the word "brother" were somehow too foreign or too precious for speech. "I know all about his so-called agent. All Sky ever wanted to do was paint. He told me he was going to leave the agency. He was going to quit." Her brows drew together angrily. "He said he just couldn't do it anymore."

Sofia searched the woman's face, recalling the words on the suicide note: *I can't do this anymore.* Officer Quimby's comments echoed in her brain: *No fingerprints on the vial or the syringe . . . Mr. Blane wasn't alone in his hotel room.* Sofia felt her stomach tighten. Was it possible that the note had been meant for Steele?

"When I heard you were still going to have the show, I wanted to see the painting." Willow June's eyes drifted lovingly to the Native American maiden on the easel. "Sky told me about it, that he had drawn it for me." She paused and said softly, "Our great-grandmother was a Sioux princess."

"And you look so much like her," Sofia said quietly.

"Perhaps I do," she acknowledged, and the smallest of smiles touched her lips.

Sofia looked up to see Rathbone Steele walking briskly toward her, curly gray head bent as if on a mission. He called out, "I need some more of those brochures I left with you, Mrs. Parker."

"You!" Willow June was on her feet, her face dark with anger. "What have you done to my brother?" she screamed, grabbing hold of his arm.

Sofia scrambled up and tried to pull Willow June back.

"My dear young woman, I have done nothing to your brother, whoever he may be." His cheeks colored as people turned to see what the commotion was all about.

"He's dead! And it's your fault!" She pulled away from Sofia's grasp and lunged at Steele, grabbing onto his suit.

He leaped back with a grace surprising for his bulk and smoothed his rumpled lapels. As Marla and several others came rushing toward them, he yelled for someone to call the authorities. "This is the deranged woman the police have been looking for!" Then, taking command of the situation, he appealed to the art show visitors. "Please, ladies and gentleman, we'll take care of this untidy situation. Don't let it spoil your appreciation of the great art available for your enjoyment."

As he and others calmed the crowd, Sofia bustled the

now-weeping Willow June into Marla's small office. "Please calm down. This won't help at all," she said, her heart pounding. She led the woman to a chair and handed her a tissue from Marla's desk.

"I'm sorry," she wailed. "But he drove Sky to do what he did. Dragging him everywhere and making him wear those ridiculous costumes. Stuff that wasn't even Sioux, just Native-looking outfits that Sky hated. They made a mockery of our real tribe. He only wanted to paint. He didn't care about the money." Gradually she settled down and blew her nose. "I hope I didn't ruin the show. You don't need to call the police. I've already identified the body. I know it's my brother."

But Sofia knew that the reason the police were looking for her involved more than making an identification of her brother. Even as the light knock sounded and Officer Quimby entered, she feared for Howahkan's lovely sister. What a shame that, after years of estrangement, their first efforts at reconciliation should end this way.

"Mrs. Hunt? Willow June Hunt?" Officer Quimby's freckled face was somber.

She looked up at him, her forehead wrinkled, eyes puzzled, and nodded.

"This is Willow June," Sofia said, as though she were making a formal introduction. "She is Skylar Blane's sister, but she—"

"I'll have to ask you to come with me, please," Officer Quimby said, ignoring Sofia. He extended his arm, keeping his gaze on Willow June.

Sofia saw the woman's confusion. There hadn't been time to tell her that the police had not ruled Howahkan's death a suicide and that they were looking for someone who might have administered a fatal dose of the victim's antidepressant and wiped the vial and syringe clean of fingerprints.

Willow June was led to the door, the officer's large hand firm on her arm. She looked back at Sofia with frightened eyes but said nothing as she was led out of the office, out of the library, and into the police car idling at the curb.

Was she as innocent as she seemed? Sofia stared after her. Was it all an act? Had she "helped" her brother to his death? If so, why had she stayed in town? Or was she, as Rathbone Steele had pronounced, deranged?

17

Omaha, Nebraska
June 1885

"The trouble at the Wild West arena and disturbing reports about Robert had led to a night of restlessness. It was with relief that Libby welcomed the radiant morning. She could hardly wait to get on her way to the arena. She had to find some way to help her new friends whose livelihoods were being threatened.

Meg was dressing slowly in the bedroom the girls shared. She pulled on a high-collared white blouse and a tan skirt of sturdy linen. "Do hurry, Meg," urged Libby, who was quite ready for the day, clad in her green riding habit.

The pensive frown on Meg's face meant she was puzzling over something.

"Are you sure this is a good idea, Libby?" she asked, securing her blond locks with a ribbon at the back of her neck.

"I don't know," Libby said truthfully. "But Buffalo Bill's show is in trouble, and we've got to help." She closed her jacket, feeling the rapid pulse in her neck as she worked the top button.

"I'm sorry," Meg said, pursing her lips. "I know what Greta said about Robert was upsetting . . ." She let the sentence drift.

"You've nothing to apologize for," Libby said, a little impatiently. She didn't want to talk about Robert. When she had declined to walk with him the night before, his displeasure had been clear. She hadn't meant to hurt him, but she no longer felt comfortable with him.

"I must ask Annie how she created that wonderful costume she wears," Libby said, wanting to change the subject. "Teddy says her family was very poor and that Annie even lived for a time in a home for orphans and mentally ill people after her father died. That's where she learned to sew."

"But she taught herself to shoot to support her family and herself," Meg said. "I read that in Sonja's magazine." She colored and reached under the bed. She pulled out a newspaperlike publication with a black-and-white heading that read *Frontier Adventures*. "It has stories about Colonel Cody too. Only he wasn't really a colonel. He got that name from scouting for General Sheridan."

Libby reached for the paper, recalling Aunt Tillie's comment about dime novels by Ned Buntline. This one had another writer's name attached to it, but as she flipped the pages, she saw that it contained tales of the frontier West and an editorial on the war.

"I've only read one story, the one about Miss Annie. Did you know she has never pointed a gun at a man? Her Quaker mother was very much against guns. But I guess she relented when Annie began winning competitions and bringing home the money she earned from them."

While Meg continued to recount what she'd read, Libby traced her finger over the lines of type. She read rapidly of General Philip Sheridan's four-year campaign against the Cheyenne and about William F. Cody receiving the Congressional Medal of Honor for his bravery as a scout for Sheridan. Statements made by both men were quoted. She cringed at "the only good Indian is a dead one," attributed to Sheridan.

Scanning the next few lines, she read Cody's comments expressing relief that the Indian Wars were ended and that he'd never killed a Native unless his life was threatened. In graphic prose, the writer detailed the victories and defeats of the Plains Wars. In one battle, an entire company was lost during an attack by renegade American Indians. Cody had not known they were in the area. The writer seemed to place great stock in being objective and considering all sides of an issue.

The writer queried: *But is he responsible? Did Cody lead these brave men into ambush as some claim? Nay, but he mourns the terrors of war and the deaths of these good men, many just boys, such as James Ealy who was but seventeen years old.*

Libby felt the hairs on the back of her neck prickle. *The writer must mean Robert's brother. How many James Ealys who died at seventeen could there be?*

A chill passed through Libby. "Meg, put this back under the bed," she ordered, suddenly breathless.

"Are you all right, Libby?" Meg's eyes widened with concern.

Libby picked up her riding crop and straightened her shoulders. "I'm fine," she said stiffly. "Now let's get going. Teddy will be waiting."

"Make sure to eat all your breakfast," Aunt Tillie ordered when they sat down at the table. "There's oatmeal, stewed tomatoes, side meat, and fresh corn bread. I'm not going to send you back to Boston looking like scarecrows. Your mother would skin me alive."

Libby smiled at the expression Aunt Tillie would never have used before moving to Nebraska. As her aunt rambled on, Libby thought about what she'd read in the magazine. *If Robert's brother was killed in a raid involving Cody, Robert might have cause to hate Sheridan's scout as well as the Indians he fought against. But would he stoop to criminal ends in his bitterness?*

"If you girls are going to be riding all over Omaha with my wrangler, you'll need your strength," Tillie said, dark eyes dancing with good humor and energy.

"Not all over Omaha," Libby said, pushing away her anxiety.

"Just to the Wild West arena." Libby blessed their good fortune that Buffalo Bill had chosen a site so near their aunt's homestead to stage his show. "And we promise to be home on time today."

"See that you do, and remember tonight is the mayor's ball. Be sure to lay your gowns out for Greta to prepare. The ladies' society has planned a grand event, and I want you to look your very best."

A persistent knock at the front of the house stopped Tillie's rhetoric. "Now who is calling at this hour of the morning?"

"Maybe Teddy with the horses," Meg suggested.

They followed their aunt out of the kitchen.

"Let's slip out past whoever is calling," Libby whispered to her sister, "and be on our way."

But she halted at the sight of a tall, bearded man grasping Teddy's shoulder with one hand. With the other he held a battered hat against his leather britches. A star gleamed against his black vest. He peered at Aunt Tillie through solemn, colorless eyes. "He work for you, ma'am?" he asked, pointing with his chin at Teddy.

Libby stared unbelieving at Teddy's milk-white face; even his freckles seemed blanched into colorlessness.

Aunt Tillie's face matched Teddy's for pallor, but her voice was stern. "He's one of my hands. What do you want with him, Sheriff?"

"Just done a search of your barn," said the sheriff. "We got a tip that he had the money from Buffalo Bill's show," said the burly man. "Found the bag in his bedroll, but the money's gone, except for a few notes. Afraid I gotta take him in, ma'am."

No, it can't be! Libby scrambled toward the sheriff, glaring. "This is a mistake. Teddy is no thief." Reaching Teddy's side, she read the anguish on his features.

"I didn't take it," Teddy said, blue eyes imploring. "I didn't take any money. I don't know how the bag got in with my stuff."

"Sing for the district judge, sonny. But if you tell us where the rest of the money is, it'll go easier for you." The sheriff turned to one side and spat on the ground.

Libby reached out a hand to comfort Teddy. "I know you didn't do this. We're going to find out who did," she said with grim determination. She turned angrily back to the sheriff, her throat dry, her voice unnaturally high. "Really, Sheriff, a man would be a fool to leave clear evidence right where anyone could find it and then hang around to get caught."

Libby's mind raced. *Teddy wouldn't betray his friends. It must have been someone else—someone like Hawk who was bitter about being let go from the Wild West show and who clearly disliked Teddy. It could be anyone wanting to run Cody and his Indians off. Maybe even Robert Ealy.* Aghast at her sudden thought, she sputtered, "Somebody is trying to frame Teddy, and they're not going to get away with it."

The sheriff shrugged and tipped his hat to a white-faced Tillie. "Sorry, ma'am. I still gotta take the boy in."

Libby watched with a sinking heart as they rode off toward town. "Colonel Cody will vouch for Teddy. You'll see," she called after them.

Tillie shook her head, distress and shame written on her face. "Robert told me I shouldn't trust Teddy."

"Teddy *didn't* do this," Libby repeated. "I know he didn't. And we're going to prove it." *And prove it to Robert Ealy too.* "Aunt Tillie, do you know where Hawk is? I mean, now that he isn't working here anymore?"

"Not working here?" She stared at Libby, her lips pursed in consternation.

Had Robert not informed Aunt Tillie about Hawk's smoking in the barn as he said he would? Maybe he hadn't gotten around to it yet, or he had decided not to tell her at all. It wasn't his business really. But as Libby considered these fleeting thoughts in the tense atmosphere, she grew more and more uneasy. Quickly she explained what she had witnessed two days earlier in the barn.

"I don't understand this at all," Tillie said. "Hawk's something of a maverick but—"

"He might have taken the money from the arena," Libby said. "He's hounded Teddy ever since he was fired from the Wild West show."

Tillie put a hand to her mouth. "This is awful." She shook her head fretfully. "I told my foreman to send all the hands out to the south pasture today. Calves have been getting through gaps in the fence. The job will take them all day, especially with Teddy gone." She blew her breath out in a long stream and narrowed her eyes. "Are you sure about this, Libby?"

"No, but the sheriff needs to know about Hawk, and we've got to tell Colonel Cody what's happened to Teddy."

"This couldn't happen at a worse time," Tillie lamented. "I'm sorry as I can be about all of this, but you know the mayor's ball is tonight. I'm counting on you girls being there too."

Libby's mind raced. What was a ball compared with helping Teddy prove his innocence? On the other hand, she mused, she had some questions for Robert. Yes, she would make sure to be there. She was more than a little eager to hear what he had to say about what had happened. "Let's get the horses, Meg," Libby said, heading quickly for the barn. "Get someone to help with the gear. I'm going to get Teddy's sketchbook. It will bring him some comfort as he sits in that jail."

She found Teddy's bedroll tossed into a corner, the lantern askew on the table. Some personal items were scattered about, but it was obvious that the sheriff hadn't needed to put much effort into his search. Whoever had hidden the bag had wanted it to be found. She looked around carefully, rifling the straw with the toe of her boot. Maybe she'd find a clue, something the sheriff overlooked.

Libby knew she'd better grab the sketchbook and charcoal sticks and get going, as Meg would be waiting with the horses in the corral. She was about to turn away when she saw something glittering in the straw—a small stickpin with a tiny white stone in the center, lodged at the base of a hay bale. Something stirred in her memory. She'd seen that unusual piece of jewelry before.

Electricity surged through her. In a flash, she remembered where—smack in the center of Robert Ealy's cravat.

Robert could have lost the pin anytime since he seemed to come and go freely in the barn, bunkhouse, and other buildings on Tillie's property.

But what if. . . ?

With trembling fingers, she tucked the pin into her reticule. She would have to think carefully about this, but right now, she had to get to the arena.

A half hour later, she and Meg tied their horses to a cotton-

wood at the edge of the Wild West grounds. The village teemed with activity. Animals were being led or curried, and wood fires tended. Children played as the adults tended to their chores.

When an attractive Native girl ducked out of a nearby teepee, Libby's throat tightened. *How can I tell her about Teddy?*

Chumani, in a simple buckskin dress, watched them with a stoic expression. A beaded headband restrained her long, straight hair, and around her neck a crucifix glittered in the sun. In one graceful hand she held a wooden pail.

"Oh, Chumani," Libby began hoarsely. "We have bad news.

It's Teddy." She swallowed. "He's been arrested."

Chumani's liquid eyes widened. As she abruptly stopped, water sloshed over the edge of her pail. She stood stock-still, watching them approach.

"The sheriff searched Aunt Tillie's barn today," Libby said. "Among Teddy's things, he found the bag stolen from the Wild West show. Only a few dollars were in it. The rest was gone." She felt her voice tremble. "I'm so sorry to tell you. But we don't believe he's guilty. Not for one second."

Chumani stared at Libby and then at Meg. In the protracted silence, the brilliant sun seemed to mock them.

"We're so sorry," Meg said into the stillness. "This, on top of losing your pet."

Chumani shook her head vigorously, as though to shake away a minor concern. But her dark eyes grew wide with alarm. "I must find my friend, my sister Annie."

Like Chumani, Annie had been adopted by Sitting Bull, though Little Missie had been chosen more recently. "May we come with you?" Libby asked, taking a step toward her.

Chumani gave an almost imperceptible nod and led the way toward the tenting area. Nearby they heard the sounds of gunshots and glass breaking.

They watched as Annie Oakley, dressed in leggings and a skirt trimmed with ribbon and embroidered flowers, set the gun down on a small, cloth-covered table next to her. Hair cascading in a rich brown stream from beneath her sombrero, she picked up a glass ball from a table and threw it into the air. She quickly picked up her shotgun, took aim, and pulled the trigger. The glass broke into a million glittering shards. Then she threw up two balls at a time, shot the first, twirled completely around, and shot the other before it hit the ground. Annie put the gun down on the table as Chumani ran toward her.

Annie peered into the stricken face. "What's wrong? Is it

Bright Eagle?"

"It's Teddy," Libby said, stepping forward. "He has been arrested. The sheriff found the money bag among his things in my aunt's barn."

Annie's eyes widened as the news registered. "Teddy?" It was clear that the idea was preposterous to her. She gave a tense little smile, studying them with a troubled frown. "You're Teddy's friends, Elizabeth and Margaret?"

"Yes. Libby and Meg," Libby said, and without taking a breath, added, "We know Teddy is innocent. We have to get him cleared of this ridiculous charge." Libby's voice broke, and she struggled to regain control. "We have to find out who really took the money and get it back."

"Of course Teddy didn't take it," Annie said angrily. "And I know he isn't responsible for all those other malicious acts either. Not Teddy."

"I saw someone," Chumani said shyly at first, then more loudly. "I saw a man that day."

Three pairs of eyes fixed themselves on Chumani. "The day the money disappeared?" Libby asked, every nerve alert.

She nodded. "I could not find Bright Eagle. I went to look for him. That is when I saw a man running away behind the office tent."

Libby stiffened. Had she seen a tall, sandy-haired gentleman in elegant dress and top hat? Would she describe Robert? Tremulously she asked, "Do you know him?"

She shook her head. "A big man with much black hair and hair here." Chumani put a finger to her lip.

Libby forced herself to sound calm as she addressed Annie. "Do you know a man who goes by the name Hawk? A roustabout who used to work here?"

Annie thought for a moment and shook her head. "So many

come and go."

Libby drew an excited breath. "He was one of my aunt's cowhands. Big, with a mustache that droops over his mouth."

Chumani nodded gravely, her eyes wide with fear. "Yes, that one."

Libby held Annie Oakley's gaze. "I think Hawk may be the one who has been causing all the trouble," she said hesitantly.

So it wasn't Robert. It was that conniving Hawk! Libby waited for relief to wash over her but felt only a gnawing sense of unease.

18

Cabot Falls, Vermont
Present Day

After Officer Quimby took Willow June away, Sofia replayed the scene in her mind. The whole thing was terribly sad. Sad that Howahkan had allowed himself to become something of a slave to his agent. Sad that he and his sister had finally reconciled, only to lose each other. As the ultimate tragedy, a fine artist was dead, and a grieving young woman might be arrested for his murder.

She was glad for the distraction of the art show. The crowds remained steady throughout the day, and she and the other volunteers had little time for anything besides responding to questions and needs, and discussing the work of Howahkan and the other artists.

Near lunchtime, Jim brought the kids, and they all went across the street for hamburgers. While the kids piled into the car to return home, Jim walked Sofia back to the library. "You've been pretty quiet," he remarked, tucking her hand into his elbow. "I guess you must be tired, or is it something else?"

She told him about Willow June's appearance, her outburst against Rathbone Steele, and the police taking her away. "I can't believe she would be involved in his death," she said. "But someone must have been there. Someone wiped fingerprints off the syringe."

Jim's features became stern, an expression he reserved for students who acted up in his classroom. After a long moment he said, "I don't like you in the middle of all this. I'm going to take the kids home, and I'll be back to get you as soon as the show is over. The police will work it out."

She kissed her husband and gave him the brightest smile she could manage before he got reluctantly into the car and drove away. She went back into the hubbub of the library, grateful for the love of her family and longing for the moment when she could fling her arms around each of them.

The attendance was brisk most of the day, but as the sun began to lower, Marla came alongside Sofia. "What a day," she said, heaving a sigh. "I worried what would happen after all the excitement over Howahkan's sister."

"Oh, Marla," Sofia said, suddenly more tired than she had ever been. "I feel terrible about it. To think she's lost her brother now, when they might have had many years to enjoy each other."

Marla pursed her lips in a disdainful expression. "Steele is holding forth as though nothing happened at all," she said grimly. "He waxes more and more philosophical as he makes each sale." She let out a long sigh and cocked her head to one side, scrutinizing Sofia. "You should take a break. You look worn out."

"I'm fine, but maybe I will step out for a breath of air. I won't be gone more than five minutes."

"Take your time," Marla said. "We can take care of things here. You've had far too much drama for one day." Marla reached for Sofia's hand and gave it an encouraging squeeze.

Sofia slipped out of the rear exit and breathed in the early evening air. It would be a good night to look up into the canopy of stars, to walk in a field of wildflowers and let the wind blow with abandon. She'd like to sit by the water like the girl in the painting and listen to the faithful lapping of the waves. In the rarefied air of nature, the little world of men and their maneuverings would vanish. Wouldn't they?

Instead, Sofia decided to take a turn around the library, ending at the little-used rear parking lot. She and Marla and a few of the volunteers had parked there to save as much room as possible at the front for guests. She checked her windows to make sure they were all the way up. Though the night looked clear, rainstorms could happen without warning.

The library's automatic lights switched on, signaling the coming dark. In their dusky light, she noticed an unfamiliar vehicle and drew closer to read the license plate. *Rathbone Steele's rental car,* she thought, frowning. The scene between the agent and Willow June played through her mind again. Howahkan's sister had a powerful dislike for Steele, lashing out in front of the crowd and blaming him for ruining her brother's life. And Steele had been quick to notify the police.

Sofia felt no kinship with Rathbone Steele, but was there any truth to his claims about Willow June's sanity? She stared at the sleek late-model sedan that couldn't have come cheap. Was there anything to Willow June's accusation? Had the agent become affluent on the earnings of a troubled young artist who only wanted to paint and had no interest in money? She thought of how Steele had marked up the prices on the paintings before Howahkan's body was even cold.

On impulse, Sofia checked the door handle on the passenger side and found that he'd been careless and left the car unlocked. Doubtless he didn't worry about theft in what he'd called the "provincial" little town of Cabot Falls. And besides, it wasn't his car.

Pushing the possible consequences from her mind, she opened the door and slipped inside. Instantly she smelled the pungent scent of his cologne. The heavy, musky odor she didn't like immediately identified the car's driver.

She glanced around the leather interior. In the backseat lay a carelessly folded newspaper. A cup from a fast-food restaurant was in one cupholder and an opened roll of candy mints was in the other. A pair of gloves were stuffed into one of the compartments. Apparently Mr. Steele was fastidious about his person but not about the car he drove. And why didn't people put gloves in the glove compartment?

She glanced back to make sure she wasn't being watched. All was quiet.

Wouldn't Steele have a fit if he knew I was sitting in his car? It would serve him right for leaving it unlocked, she thought. She wrinkled her nose and considered opening the door to relieve the nauseating sweetness of his cologne. She fished around idly in the cubbyholes and door pockets but found only a bit of discarded paper from his candy mints.

Wouldn't it be something if she found a cuff link with a missing pearl? She shook her head at her own audacity. *You need to get out and mind your own business,* she told herself sternly.

But her gaze kept returning to the glove compartment.

With shaky fingers, Sofia pushed the release button, and the little door fell open. The light inside the box revealed the usual assortment of papers, including the vehicle user's manual and insurance information. She pulled them out and put them on her lap while she searched the box for stray objects, hoping to find a cuff link missing a small white pearl. But there was nothing.

Sofia took a deep breath and leafed through the documents to find the rental agreement. There it was, with Rathbone Steele's signature. She checked the date, and her pulse began to jump. He had rented this car on Tuesday evening at eight thirty, not on Thursday.

Tuesday. That meant he could have been in Cabot Falls on Wednesday, the day Howahkan had died.

Could he have flown in to Boston twice, once on Tuesday and again on Thursday to provide an alibi for himself? He had presented satisfactory proof of his whereabouts, but Steele was a clever man. It wouldn't be difficult to produce a second airline ticket.

If he had been here earlier, he could have been with Howahkan the night he died.

The driver's-side door flew open, and the car was flooded with light. Sofia's heart leaped into her throat.

"Breaking and entering, Mrs. Parker?" The gravelly voice of Rathbone Steele intruded like a thunderbolt.

She clutched the papers in her lap with trembling fingers and stared as he climbed in and shut the door.

"May I ask exactly what you think you're doing?" He spoke with what seemed careful control, but the eyes beneath the bushy brows betrayed his anger.

She smoothed the documents and replaced them in their envelope without speaking. Praying for calm, she quietly put them back in the glove compartment and closed it. Darkness descended except for shadowy light from the building behind them. She made no move to run but simply folded her hands in her lap as the cloying sweetness of his cologne assaulted her.

"I know you were here," she said without looking at him.

There was a lull of heart-pounding silence.

"I haven't the slightest idea what you're talking about, and I'm incensed that my privacy has been invaded. I'm sure the police will want to know its citizens engage in breaking and—"

"Yes," she interrupted. "Let's call the police. I'm sure they'll be interested to know that you rented this car two days before you admitted to being in Cabot Falls." She turned to face him in the shadowy light, wondering where this sudden burst of courage was coming from.

He glared at her, the pupils of his almond-shaped eyes black and glittering. Without speaking, he raised his eyebrows and set his mouth in a grim line.

She could hear the slight catch in his breath and then the click of the door locks. She scrambled to reach the release button on the passenger side but found the effort fruitless. He had engaged the child locks on the driver's panel.

"Unlock this door," she demanded.

Her heart thudded in her chest as the rental car's engine roared to life. "Stop and let me out this minute!" she yelled at him. "I'm not going anywhere with you."

He pressed the gas pedal and zoomed out of the parking lot and onto the street, swerving around a red pickup and a slow-moving Mercedes.

"I'm afraid you are not in a position to demand anything, Mrs. Parker." He nudged closer to the car ahead of him until only a hairsbreadth remained between them. His audible breathing accelerated, and his knuckles turned white on the steering wheel.

"Where are you taking me?" she shouted. Then, forcing herself to be calm, she added, "My husband will be coming to pick me up any minute. He'll come after you. The others will be looking for me too. You can't get away with this." *And what is "this"? What is he going to do with me?* Her thoughts tumbled crazily over one another.

"Shut up."

The words, so foreign to Rathbone Steele's usual cultured vocabulary, felt like a slap. Sofia drew in her breath. She saw that he was fighting for calm, thinking hard what he should do now that he had foolishly left his car unlocked with damning evidence inside. She waited, her heart beating hard even as her anger mounted. "What were you doing in town on Wednesday?" she asked.

"Just because I was here doesn't mean anything." He veered around a corner and headed out of town. "I don't have to explain my whereabouts to you. There are any number of reasons for an earlier arrival."

"But only one that explains why you lied about it," she shot back. "And besides, I know you were there. I found the pearl." Then, without considering it for more than a second, she added, "The one you lost in his room." His face, averted in the shadowy interior, paled in the lights of an oncoming car. She was sure she saw him stiffen.

He continued to drive along the road. Where was he taking her? Were they looking for her yet? She'd told Marla she wouldn't be more than five minutes. Many more had passed. *If only I could reach over and honk the horn . . . draw attention somehow.*

But how was she to accomplish that? Rathbone suddenly pulled off the road and brought the car to a shuddering stop. "Let me out," Sofia said. "I'll walk back, and you can go on."

"I don't think so, Mrs. Parker." Then he fell quiet, his eyes trained on the windshield.

"I won't say anything," she said, now on the edge of panic. He had to know the police didn't have any evidence to convict him or they would have arrested him by now. She was the only one who had seen the second rental agreement. She was a decided liability. Was he crazy enough or evil enough to silence her permanently?

Rathbone Steele continued to stare into the night. He hadn't refuted her accusation about the pearl. He'd made no comment about it at all. What was he thinking?

"This doesn't have to go any further," she said. "Maybe you didn't mean to do it. Maybe it was all a terrible mistake." Could she appeal to some higher nature in the man? But he seemed distracted and distant, his jaw rigid.

The raspy voice suddenly cut through her panic. "He was going to quit me," he said as he stared into the glass. "After all I did for him."

Sofia held her breath. The note, the torn-off scrap found at the hotel. It had been meant for Steele. Howahkan had written it to his agent, in a desperate attempt to free himself. Steele must have torn off the portion with his name on it and left it, knowing the authorities would think it a suicide note.

Cars passed them by on the road. If only she could break away or alert someone to her peril!

"He was nothing when I found him," Steele went on in that strange, singsong babble. "A penniless wannabe, pining away in an old attic. I got him a decent place to live. I taught him how to make money with his talent. I took care of him when he had nobody. Got him help when he wanted to kill himself." He cocked his head to one side, as if hearing a voice from somewhere. "He wanted to die. I just helped him along."

Chills ravaged Sofia. She imagined him coolly injecting a lethal dose of the antidepressant into the young man's body. Was he crazy?

Headlights from more cars appeared behind them. Steele, absorbed with whatever demons drove him, didn't seem to notice.

"He owed me," came the voice, angry now. "I made him famous. He owed me, and he'll pay." Steele paused and turned to look at Sofia, a trace of a smile on his lips. "And now that he's dead, I'll make him more famous than ever."

Suddenly a car swerved around them on the left and came to a screeching halt, hemming them in.

Sofia lurched at Steele, who was still dazed. She reached over him and pressed the child lock button before he could react.

More headlights blazed in front and behind as several cars converged on them, two of them with flashing red and blue lights.

Marla must have called for help when she noticed Steele and I were missing.

The door of the car ahead of them flew open, and Jim leaped toward them. He flung Steele's door wide. Like a blond avenging angel, Jim grabbed the stunned agent, pulled him out of the car, and threw him to the ground.

19

Omaha, Nebraska
June 1885

Learning that Hawk had been seen the night the Wild West's money was stolen, the four friends decided to split up to ferret out more clues and find the guilty party. Annie and Libby went to the arena to find Colonel Cody while Meg and Chumani brought Teddy's drawing supplies to the jail.

Annie Oakley, still dressed in her Wild West costume, went into the arena office and came back with the Colonel. The show's manager, Nate Salsbury, walked alongside him. Cody looked fatigued, though elegant in a double-breasted suit and bright red shirt. His long hair, which he usually wore loose and flowing, was tied back.

"It's Miss Elizabeth, isn't it?" He made a formal bow. "Little Missie says you have come to see me. I am honored."

"The sheriff arrested Teddy this morning," Libby began, not waiting for any more formalities. "They found the Wild West's receipt bag in his bedroll, but there was little money in it. And he didn't take it." Libby rushed on. "Chumani saw someone else running from the office here the day of the theft."

Cody's gaze sharpened.

"We think it could be a man called Hawk who works for my aunt. He used to be employed here as a roustabout."

Cody looked puzzled and turned to Salsbury for confirmation.

"I had to let that one go a few weeks back," said the dignified, balding man as he stroked his pointed beard. "His brother asked us to take him back, said he'd be accountable for him, but the bloke was a troublemaker."

"Once Nate makes up his mind, there's no changing it," Cody said knowingly.

"Brother?" Libby asked in a small voice.

"Good-looking man, a fancy dresser," the manager said. "Liked to push his weight around."

A smile lit Cody's face. "Wasn't he the man with you at the auditorium the night I came out shooting and shocked everyone at the concert? I gave you a couple of passes as I recall," he said.

Libby stiffened. *He means Robert. Of course, but a brother? Robert said he lost his brother, James, in an Indian attack.* She had assumed he had meant his only brother. A fragment of conversation leaped to mind. *Mr. Ealy always chooses Hawk to handle his carriage when he comes to the ranch.*

"I didn't know Hawk had a brother." Libby's pulse was racing. *Was it true?* She was beginning to doubt everything she knew about Robert Ealy, and to wonder if he and Hawk could be working together. Both had motives to cause trouble for Buffalo Bill.

Salsbury straightened his shoulders and nodded politely. "Sorry about Teddy," he said. "I liked him."

Libby and Annie exchanged anxious glances as the manager and Cody headed back into the tent.

"Hawk must be somewhere around your aunt's place. And the money too," Annie said. "Why don't we have a look? I'll go with you."

"We'll be able to check out the bunkhouse without interruption," Libby said. "Aunt Tillie sent all the hands to the south pasture today. No one will be around."

Riding sidesaddle and armed with new clues about the stolen money, Libby and Annie headed for the homestead. Annie's rifle was firmly secured in her saddle scabbard.

Not bad to have the Peerless Lady Wing Shot of the West at your side when you're heading into danger, Libby thought. Then she wondered what kind of trouble they were about to encounter.

The long bunkhouse on Aunt Tillie's ranch lay beyond the barn and corral; it seemed to be deserted. They rode in quietly, bringing their horses in from the west and securing them to the fence rails of the corral.

The air inside the bunkhouse was hot and still, the plank floor dusty, and the furnishings spare. Wooden partitions that only reached three-quarters of the way to the ceiling divided the room into sections, providing a modicum of privacy for the men.

"We're not likely to find anything in here," Libby whispered, not knowing why she was whispering.

"Yes, if Hawk took the money, he'd be more likely to bury it outside somewhere," Annie agreed. She propped her rifle against a wall. "But he may not have had time yet."

They searched carefully, peering under cots, blankets, and old crates, but they stopped at the sound of hoofbeats.

"Someone's coming!" Libby exclaimed.

She ducked behind the first wooden partition. Annie ran toward another and then, remembering the rifle, went back for it, returning only a second before the door opened and Hawk stepped in.

Libby held her breath as the big man lumbered to the far side of the room, stopped, and cast a wary glance around him. His rumpled black hair bunched out in all directions around a face like soiled leather. Making a half turn to the right, he bent down and lifted a floorboard neatly from its mooring. With both hands he scooped up the dirt beneath the floor.

When he pulled out a square burlap pouch, Libby had no doubt about its contents. She jumped out from behind the partition, her long skirts stirring up dust. "Thief!" she yelled. "I knew it was you."

Hawk swung around, coal-like eyes bulging with surprise. He struggled up, dropping the pouch. "So the fancy lady is a snoop. You got no business in here," he said with steely reserve.

"And you have no business taking the Wild West's money," Libby said. "Time for you to own up and get Teddy out of jail."

Hawk sneered and a harsh bubble of laughter ripped the air. "I don't think so," he scoffed, then lunged toward her.

At that second, Annie stepped out from her hiding place, gun drawn. "I wouldn't do that if I were you." Her voice was like tempered steel, her hand sure, as all five feet of the Peerless Lady Wing Shot of the West confronted a stunned and stuttering Hawk. He, of course, had no idea that the morally upright Annie Oakley, raised in a Quaker home, had never pointed a gun at a human being with intent to harm before that moment.

Eerie silence reigned inside the bunkhouse, and then a voice rang out. "If the best sharpshooter in the world doesn't get you, I will."

Libby whirled around to see Aunt Tillie dressed in a ball gown of mauve silk and a pair of Hector's old working boots. The rifle at her shoulder was pointed straight at Hawk's head.

"I did a little snooping of my own," she said, not taking her eyes off the astonished Hawk. "When I saw the girls ride up, I took the liberty of sending for the sheriff. He'll be riding in any minute, which is a good thing because we ladies have a ball to attend. I've arranged for a carriage. Should be here in an hour or so. So I'm going to keep this coyote cornered until the sheriff arrives while my nieces get ready. I believe I hear him now."

Libby laughed with relief. Aunt Tillie wouldn't halt her social planning, even at a desperate moment like this.

Moments later, the sheriff arrived to haul off the belligerent man, who was loudly protesting his innocence. Libby wondered how long it would take for him to name his accomplice. She was pretty certain he had one—specifically a fair-haired gentleman who owned a silver cravat pin with a pearly stone. She thought she could feel the small bump it made inside her reticule where it lay hidden. But first she had to be sure. Robert had no idea his plan had been blown apart. He'd be all style and gentility at the dance.

"My partner, Frank, and I are invited to the auditorium tonight," Annie whispered to Libby before preparing to ride back to the arena. "I'll see you there. And Libby, be careful."

20

Omaha, Nebraska
June 1885

*I*n a stylish rented carriage Libby, Meg, and Aunt Tillie arrived at the auditorium, where the freestanding seats had been cleared away. Kerosene lanterns posted at each of the many windows shone golden on the oaken floor. Music from an ensemble of strings and woodwinds carried lively music on the evening air.

Libby wore her blue satin gown with delicate ribbon edging that Greta had readied for her while she had been out. She had dressed with amazing speed, but she was glad they were a bit late for the festivities. People were already dancing and mingling around refreshment tables at the perimeter of the hall. The tone was festive, the decorations cheery. If only it could be a real party without the specter of deceit and ill will hovering in the wings.

Annie Oakley and her husband and manager, Frank Butler, arrived and were quickly surrounded by curious guests, including an admiring and doting Mayor Quaid. If anyone had expected a graceless tomboy, they were amazed at the vision of feminine beauty she presented in a lavender silk gown with lacy embroidery along a modest V-neck. Her chestnut hair was artfully swept off her neck, revealing ears adorned with tiny gold earrings.

She can fit in anywhere, Libby thought admiringly. Who

would believe she had been born Phoebe Ann Moses on a bleak Ohio farm and had overcome poverty, prejudice, physical setbacks, and shyness to become the best-known sharpshooter in the West?

"I suppose I was born with the ability to shoot," she had told Libby.

The more Libby learned about Annie, the more she admired her. In the best Quaker tradition, she put family first and regarded the sanctity of life highly. With money she'd earned from hunting while she lived with her mother, she had been able to pay off the family mortgage. It was also known that she sent money to orphans at the Darke County Infirmary in Ohio, where she had worked for a brief time.

Libby caught Annie's eye and was rewarded with a conspiratorial wink. They both knew there was a long way to go before the evening ended.

It wasn't long before Robert Ealy found Libby sitting with Meg near their aunt, who was as yet unaware of their suspicions about the promising young nephew of Mayor Quaid. Libby was surprised when Aunt Tillie took her suddenly by the arm and whisked her away to introduce her to some friends just as Robert started toward them. Was Aunt Tillie having second thoughts about Libby and the mayor's nephew?

Libby responded to casual questions and small talk from excited guests and soon found herself taking the arm of a darkhaired young man with dove-gray eyes and long lashes. The ensemble began the strains of Johann Strauss's *Blue Danube*.

The young man was an excellent dancer, and Libby could imagine herself getting lost in the lovely melody and freedom of movement. But suddenly Robert appeared, and her partner released her with a gracious bow.

Robert said nothing immediately but placed his arm around

her waist and guided her in step with the romantic music. His hand felt warm and slightly damp in hers, and she was aware of a certain rigidity. Maybe he was nervous, or perhaps her apprehension was showing. She hoped he couldn't feel the rapid beating of her heart.

After a few moments, she heard his throaty voice in her ear. "You kept me waiting a long time tonight, Miss Elizabeth. You were late, and then you were surrounded by Tillie's friends."

She didn't like his use of her aunt's first name, as though they were old acquaintances of a similar age. "Sorry to inconvenience you," she said, and when he moved back a little, she realized that he had heard the edge in her voice. She sniffed and held her head more erect. "I was rather busy this afternoon, as it happens."

When he didn't respond, she continued. "You'll be interested to know that the sheriff has arrested someone for stealing the money from the Wild West arena."

His reply was calm and measured. "Yes, your aunt told me of Teddy's arrest. Most unfortunate, but these drifters are simply not—"

"Oh, that's old news." She broke in rather more smugly than she'd intended. "Teddy wasn't the thief. It was Hawk who was arrested. He had the money buried under the floor of the bunkhouse."

She felt him stiffen. His complexion became ghostly in the light of the gas lamps. "I see," he mumbled, taking a few jerky steps.

"Mind you, he was still declaring his innocence as the sheriff hauled him away. Says he was just following orders. I expect he'll break down in due course and tell the authorities all about it. Actually," she went on, twisting the mental knife even further, "something else turned up in the stable. It probably belongs to whoever was in with Hawk on the theft." Libby paused for a brief moment before remarking, "Oh, the music is coming to an end."

Robert dropped her hand, stood quite still, and managed a half smile. "I'm certain it will all be sorted out soon enough." He led her off the floor and gave a little bow. His voice sounded stiff and unnatural. "Thank you for the dance."

Annie swept toward her from across the room. "Is everything all right?" she asked, guiding Libby toward a more secluded spot.

"I think the man I just danced with is connected to the theft," Libby said in a hushed voice, "and probably the accidents at the arena."

"The brother Mr. Salsbury described?"

"I don't know if he's any relation at all, but I think he used Hawk to get back at Colonel Cody. He believes Cody led his brother's regiment into an ambush. James was killed in the massacre, and Robert has hated the colonel ever since."

Annie's soft brown eyes narrowed. "An angry man is a dangerous man."

Libby patted the small reticule hidden in the folds of her dress. "I found his cravat pin in Teddy's quarters in the stable. I think he dropped it when he put the money bag in Teddy's bedroll." She looked across the room to where she had seen Robert a few minutes before, looking uncomfortable between the mayor and Aunt Tillie. Now he was nowhere to be seen. She turned back to Annie. "When I told Robert, he became very agitated."

"He knows you have it?" Annie asked incredulously.

"I only said that something else had been found near Teddy's bunk, but I think he knows."

"Libby, we've got to tell the sheriff." They locked eyes, and then in one joint move, wove their way through the dancing crowd to the exit. "We'll take my buggy. I'll explain to Frank later." She ran to the hitching area, hoisting up her lavender skirts, with Libby following closely behind.

Are we crazy? They rode across the plains in fancy ball gowns, skirts billowing in the wind, hair streaming behind them. Every nerve in Libby's body tingled with excitement as the silver moon lit the prairie.

They had covered most of the distance to the sheriff's office when galloping hooves sounded behind them. Libby spun around on the buggy seat.

Robert, tall and hatless, his black coat flapping in the wind, spurred the big black horse forward. He bore down on them, a pistol clutched in his right hand.

What was he doing, and how did he hope to get away with it? Had his vendetta against Cody made him crazy?

"Robert's coming!" Libby choked out. "And he's got a gun."

"Everyone—cowboy or gentleman—wears one in this wild country," Robert had told her that when they were resting under the cottonwood tree and his coat had fallen open to reveal the gun in its holster.

Suddenly a shot rang out. Libby cringed, her heart hammering. Did he intend to kill them?

Annie urged the gelding forward, but the horse and buggy were no match for Robert's powerful steed. The distance between them closed. He swung around in front of the whinnying, shuddering gelding, halting it in its tracks. The carriage lurched to a stop in a cloud of dust.

"Don't!" Robert yelled as Annie reached for her rifle, which had fallen to the floor. A platinum specter in the moonlight, Robert ordered them to get out of the buggy. His ice-blue eyes flashed.

As she scrambled down, Libby saw Robert's face suddenly blanch. He stared at her, then at Annie. His mouth fell open and quickly closed. Had he expected a compliant Meg out for a drive with her sister? Instead, he found himself facing the world's most famous sharpshooter, but sadly, one with no weapon in hand.

"What do you want?" Annie demanded coolly, drawing herself up to her full five-foot height. "Apart from ruining my dress, that is?" She opened a fold of fabric to reveal a round hole. Robert's shot had gone wide, as he perhaps intended, catching Annie's billowing lavender skirt.

"I'm sorry to interrupt your moonlight ride, ladies," he said with mock politeness. But his glare was anything but friendly. "If you will kindly return my property, you may go on your way."

"We don't know what you're talking about," Annie said vehemently.

The gun waved dangerously in his hand. "Miss Elizabeth knows exactly what I mean," he said through tightly clenched teeth.

The cravat pin burned through the reticule beneath Libby's gown. At the thought of Robert's hands clutching her, wrenching away his coveted prize, she shuddered. Then slowly, deliberately, she opened her reticule and pulled out the glittering pin.

With a prayer for divine guidance, she lifted her arm and threw it as hard as she could into the dusty road.

Startled, Robert jumped back, stumbling into the great black horse. It reared and bellowed, knocking the man to the ground and sending the pistol flying.

In a flash, Annie scooped up the gun. "Stay down!" she yelled at Robert as he struggled to get up. She trained the pistol on him. "Get the sheriff, Libby."

"But—"

"Go," Annie said. "It's less than a mile away." Glaring at Robert, she said, "I'll put a hole in your dark heart if you move so much as a hair."

Robert Ealy couldn't know that Annie Oakley fired her gun only at clay pigeons, not people. Nor could he imagine that Boston-groomed Elizabeth Carson would expertly grip the reins and launch the buggy into the night as though she were born to it.

21

Omaha, Nebraska
June 1885

"The good china, please, Greta," Aunt Tillie said. "This is a special occasion, and we will have only the best." With one of Greta's aprons tied over her green afternoon gown, she cleared a space on the wide oval table for the china and silver service.

"We shall have the raisin cakes with vanilla sauce and the petit fours from Hansen's Bakery. Sonja, bring more cream please." Tillie bustled about the parlor, her domineering tones laced with excitement and good humor.

It was a bright Sunday in the grand parlor, only hours after the harrowing race across the plains, Robert's humiliating arrest, and Teddy's subsequent release.

Annie Oakley, in a soft, ivory-colored blouse and long pleated skirt, sat in a Queen Anne chair. Having laid aside her hat with its six-pointed star, she wore her long chestnut hair draped softly over petite shoulders. On the chintz-covered horsehair settee next to her, Libby described again how Annie had snatched Robert Ealy's gun and held him captive until the sheriff came.

"I couldn't have done it had you not thrown the pin into the road," Annie said warmly. "It took the sheriff and his men awhile to find it, I'd wager."

"But even without the pin, Hawk identified Robert as his partner," Meg broke in.

"It was all Robert's idea," Libby said. A subtle sadness edged into her anger at the man who'd deceived them all. "He and Hawk wanted to ruin Cody to avenge their brother's death, and Robert also played on Hawk's resentment at being fired from the Wild West show."

"But it was war. That wasn't Cody's fault," Meg said. "Those renegades were waiting in ambush. There was nothing he could do."

Libby turned to Aunt Tillie. "How did you know we were in the bunkhouse with Hawk?"

"I've been keeping my eye on him. He's a troublemaker, like you said, Libby dear. I found out he's been fired from half a dozen spreads from Kansas to Wyoming. When you and Miss Oakley rode up, I figured you might need some help." She gave Libby and Annie fond looks. "I may be a lady of breeding, but I've learned to handle a skunk when I smell one."

When she fell silent and sadness shadowed her face, Libby guessed her aunt was thinking of Robert Ealy, a skunk she had not recognized. It was easy to be fooled by such handsome looks, social status, and gracious manners. Libby felt a stab of regret for the man she, too, had admired. But he had allowed his losses to overwhelm his spirit. He had stooped to larceny and had endangered the lives of others.

Self-recrimination bloomed on Aunt Tillie's face. "To think I tried to match you up with that scoundrel." She shook her salt-and-pepper curls and wrung her hands.

"Aunt Tillie, he had us all fooled," Libby said, trying to soothe her.

But the regretful woman would not be comforted.

"He might have killed you, chasing after you and Miss Oakley," she lamented.

"But his shot went wide," Libby said. "He was only trying to scare us to get us to stop."

"Not wide enough," Annie broke in with a wry smile. Then she drew out a small packet from inside her shapely boot and handed it to Libby. "This is for you to remember me by."

"I shall need no token to remember you," Libby said softly, warming to the friend she would always hold in her heart. Unfolding the bit of thin paper, she found a generous swatch of lavender fabric the color of the ball gown Annie had worn the night before. The piece was carefully cut to the size of a quilt block. Libby stared in amazement at the round hole the bullet had left in the silk. "I will treasure this," she said and leaned over to hug the Peerless Lady Wing Shot of the West.

Aunt Tillie stood and placed her hands on her hips. "Where is that boy?" she demanded. "And why isn't he here?"

"Who, Aunt Tillie?" Meg asked.

"Teddy, of course," Tillie said, as though the question were completely inane.

"I suspect he's out in the barn," Libby said quietly. She knew for a fact that Chumani was with him. No doubt the two were happily celebrating Teddy's release and the arrests of Hawk and Robert Ealy. Besides the good news about Teddy, Chumani had another reason to be happy. Her old dog, Bright Eagle, had limped into camp, ragged and hungry, but sound.

"Well, what's he doing out there when the party's in here?" Aunt Tillie demanded.

"He's with Chumani," Libby stated flatly, not daring to think that her aunt's hospitality would extend to an American Indian girl.

She was stunned when Aunt Tillie called, "Sonja, go get those two. We can't possibly eat all this raisin cake without their help."

They appeared in the parlor a few moments later. Teddy looked weary but happy as he smoothed his cowlicky red hair and shifted his weight from foot to foot. Chumani stood behind him, seemingly poised for flight should she not be welcome.

Libby and Meg both leaped to their feet to greet them. Meg indicated a chair close to Annie's for Teddy, and Libby guided Chumani to the settee, sitting down next to her. Greta and Sonja plied them instantly with cake and cups of tea.

"So, young man," Tillie said, "I think you've earned a raise. I'll have the foreman see to it. Now eat." She turned suddenly on her heel and left the room, only to return seconds later carrying one of Duchess's puppies in her arms. She went straight to Chumani with a gracious smile. "I understand you are fond of dogs. Maybe you would be willing to give this little one a home. He's been bred of fine aristocratic stock. He'll make a good bird dog too, since your Bright Eagle may be too old to hunt now."

Chumani's dark eyes glistened as she took the wriggling puppy and cuddled it against her smooth cheek.

"I am grateful," she said softly. She lifted wide brown eyes to Libby. "Also, I thank you for what you did for me and my father, Sitting Bull. He does not always speak what is in his heart. I speak for both of us." It was the longest speech Libby had ever heard from Chumani, and also the longest time Aunt Tillie had ever remained quiet.

Later, when the guests were gone, Libby and Meg sat watching the sunset through the parlor window. Rosy ribbons threaded the blue-gray skies and deepened the gold in the vast fields stretching across the horizon.

"The summer will be over so soon," Meg said. "I shall miss Aunt Tillie and Teddy and Chumani and Miss Oakley." She pushed back a stray lock of wheat-colored hair. "I shall always remember Greta's wonderful cooking, and Sonja said she would write to me."

Libby nodded, but her heart was too full for speech.

Meg turned her soft gaze on her sister. "I'm sorry," she said, bowing her head over her steepled fingers. "About Robert. I think he truly cared for you."

Insightful, tender Meg. Libby let her breath out slowly.

Robert may have cared for her, but his resentment had turned friendship sour. Maybe someday he would learn from his mistake and accept the precious gift of life he'd been given.

She felt herself smiling suddenly and reached over to take Meg's hand in hers. Whatever lay ahead in her future, she was going to cherish her own gift of life. She wouldn't waste a minute of it.

22

Cabot Falls, Vermont
Present Day

It was Sunday afternoon, and Sofia and her sisters were relaxing in the four-season room, sipping cups of coffee. Jim did the serving, complete with a linen towel over his arm as he brought in a tray of biscotti. He set it down on the table, gave Sofia an indulgent grin, and left the room.

"Tell us," Gina said. "How did your marvelous husband find you and overpower that crooked agent?" Her eyes were wide with excitement. She and Rosa had dropped their Sunday schedules and rushed to Cabot Falls after hearing of their sister's perilous Saturday-night adventure.

Sofia smiled, warmth spreading through her as she recalled how Jim had burst into Rathbone Steele's car and yanked him to the ground. When Sofia hadn't returned to the library after nearly ten minutes, Marla had gone to check on her. Seeing Steele's rental car gone from the lot, she had immediately become suspicious.

"Her first phone call was to Officer Quimby," Sofia said. "Then she called Jim, who was already on his way to pick me up. He didn't hesitate one second. He had a bad feeling about Steele from the first minute he met him. Jim was practically right behind us and saw us park on the side of the road."

"You must have been terrified after Steele confessed that he did it!" Rosa exclaimed. "Why did he? Do it, I mean?"

"Howahkan was going to end his relationship with him. Steele had been taking advantage of his depression and vulnerability. He had him jumping through all kinds of hoops that made a mockery of his Native American heritage. The suicide note was really part of a letter Howahkan was writing to Steele."

"How did you know the pearl was his?" Gina wanted to know.

"I didn't," Sofia said. "But I had seen him wearing cuff links with pearls on them."

"Clever girl," Rosa said, shaking her head slowly. "You took a big risk."

"I'd already shown my hand with the rental car agreement," Sofia said. "Officer Quimby has the document now. It will prove he had opportunity. A further search will most likely turn up the cuff link with the missing pearl. That, along with Willow June's testimony and others', will convict him." She drew a deep breath, feeling profoundly sad for Skylar Blane.

Vanessa stepped into the room with a coffeepot to refill their cups. "Need anything, Mom?" she asked, luminous eyes on Sofia.

"Thanks," Sofia said, holding her cup out for a refill. "Honey, would you mind going upstairs and finding Nonna's diary? There's something I want to show Aunt Rosa and Aunt Gina."

When she had left the room, Gina said, "Now that Rathbone Steele's out of the picture, I wonder what will happen to the rest of Howahkan's paintings?"

"I think we can rely on his sister to handle that." Sofia recalled Willow June's account of reconciling with her brother after years of estrangement. "That's one good thing that's come out of all this," she said softly. "Theodore Blane would be proud of his great-granddaughter and of Skylar too, happy that his sketches led to such grand paintings that preserve their history."

"Theodore Blane?" Rosa asked. "Isn't that the young cowboy you told us about? The one who brought the two young Victorian girls to the Wild West show and introduced them to Buffalo Bill?"

"Yes. They called him Teddy. It's really an amazing coincidence, isn't it? That after all these years, his great-grandson should show up in Cabot Falls? But what I want to show you is connected with Annie Oakley, the sharpshooter who was part of Buffalo Bill's Wild West and a friend of Teddy's. I finished the entry last night. I couldn't sleep, so I read the rest of the story."

When Vanessa returned with the diary, everyone gathered close around Sofia as she read the account of the daring young woman who stunned audiences with her shooting prowess. "The hole in the lavender silk swatch was deliberately worked into the quilt to represent an 'Annie Oakley.' That's what a free pass to Cody's Wild West show was called. The Colonel gave one to Libby and Meg."

Sofia paused and then explained. "The free pass had to look different from a paid ticket, so it was punched with holes like the playing cards Annie shot at and then threw into the audience as souvenirs. The term caught on in theater, baseball, and circus worlds, and a free pass became known as an Annie Oakley. The term is part of the legend that still surrounds her. That's what the quilt has in it today—an Annie Oakley."

"I bet the lavender silk is from the dress Annie wore to the party with Libby and Meg when she was chasing that fancy enemy of the Wild West show," Vanessa said. "I can imagine her riding through the countryside with her ball gown flowing out behind her."

"She was certainly a brave young woman," Rosa declared, flinging an arm around Sofia's shoulder. "Just like our Sofia. Nonna couldn't have entrusted the quilt to anyone more perfect for it!"

Learn more about Annie's fiction books at

AnniesFiction.com

- Access your e-books
- Discover exciting new series
- Read sample chapters
- Watch video book trailers
- Share your feedback

We've designed the Annie's Fiction website especially for you!

Plus, manage your account online!

- Check your account status
- Make payments online
- Update your address

Visit us at AnniesFiction.com